GAYDONIA

GAYDONIA

A novel
by

GARY PEDLER

Adelaide Books
New York / Lisbon
2020

GAYDONIA
A novel
By Gary Pedler

Copyright © by Gary Pedler
Cover design © 2020 Adelaide Books

Published by Adelaide Books, New York / Lisbon
adelaidebooks.org

Editor-in-Chief
Stevan V. Nikolic

For any information, please address Adelaide Books
at info@adelaidebooks.org

or write to:

Adelaide Books
244 Fifth Ave. Suite D27
New York, NY, 10001

ISBN: 978-1-953510-15-0
Printed in the United States of America

Contents

Chapter 1

After the long winter of the Balkan highlands, this was the day when no one in Zablvacia could doubt that spring had arrived at last. In the country's capital – which, with an economy typical of this thrifty people, was also called Zablvacia – the sunlight poured down the steeply pitched roof of St. Stephan's Cathedral, gleamed on the silver domes of the Eastern Orthodox Church and the tiled minaret of the Mosque. At the west end of the valley where the city lay stood its one great eyesore, the Pluzinova Cookie Factory. Still, in this magical spring light, its smokestack might be taken for another minaret.

The streets of the city were thronged with cyclists and a sprinkling of beaten-up cars. Pedestrians crowded the sidewalks. It might have seemed as if every single inhabitant were out of doors, rejoicing at his release from winter's icy grip. In truth, this wasn't the case. As the clock in the tower of the Town Hall struck three, if an observer had climbed winding Gundulićeva Street and peeked through the windows of the ground floor flat of Number 35, he would have found the entire Matošić family assembled in their cramped living room. Davor Matošić occupied the boxy ancient armchair, while his wife Marija, their daughter Nevenka, and their son Ivo were squeezed together on the sofa across from him. Davor's widowed mother, Vuksa Ćuruvija, stood by the heavy oak sideboard.

Not only was the family hidden away indoors, they sat in silence. Some words spoken moments before still reverberated through the room like the last chime from the clock tower. Their vibration seemed to affect Davor the most. Davor was a big, bulky, dark-haired man in his early forties. He had a broad nose, large ears, and thick eyebrows, his mouth the only small-scale thing about him. Worry was forming pouches beneath his eyes, while the large quantities of food he ate to quiet his worrying had made a good start on a second chin below his first. Bending forward, he ran the tips of his fingers up and down his temples, as if to help him think what to do about the latest care to come his way.

It was Vuksa who spoke at last. "Goodness," she said, "this is turning into quite a long pause."

Marija opened her mouth, on the point of speaking, then refrained. Nevenka shrank down into her over-sized sweater, as if wishing she could disappear. Ivo took a deep breath in, then let it out. Davor rubbed the sides of his head even harder.

As for Vuksa, she drummed her long crimson fingernails on the sideboard. Despite a face deeply carved by an eventful life, and a hand which that morning had been even shakier than usual in applying her make-up, traces of a great lady of the stage remained in her bearing.

"Pauses can be so effective in the theater," she said. "I believe the longest pause in my operatic career occurred in the role of Mlada in *The Serpent Bridegroom* – that wheezing, but still ride-able warhorse by our greatest Zablvacian com-poser, Božidar Horvat. The pause came during the wedding scene. When the priest asked me if I took the dashing Count Granic to be my husband, you could have heard a pin drop while the audience waited for my answer. The head of a pin, even."

Vuksa picked up the decanter of walnut brandy. Although her hand still trembled slightly, thanks to the bodily control imparted by years of theatrical training, she poured herself a glass without spilling a drop. Holding it up, Vuksa asked, "Would anyone else care for one? It's a little early to imbibe, I know. Still, under the circumstances. . ."

Suddenly, Davor whipped his brown eyes toward his wife. "Did you know, Marija?" he shot out.

Marija avoided his gaze. Her skin was smooth and tawny, her black hair fell straight to her shoulders.

"Of course you did," Davor said. "You're a psychologist, after all. You see through us like panes of glass."

"I didn't see through Ivo." Marija spoke in that calm, steady voice her patients found usually reassuring, sometimes maddening. "I just saw him, saw how he was behaving. Then I asked him, and he told me."

"Ha! He told you, but you said nothing to me."

"We agreed it wasn't the right time. Ivo was just about to leave for his year of study abroad."

"And now is the right time, today of all days?"

"He'd waited so long, he had to tell you the moment he returned from the United States."

Vuksa poured another glass of brandy and held it out to Davor. "Davor, take just a few sips, to help you relax." When he ignored her, she shrugged and took a sip from the glass herself, having already finished her own.

Davor turned his fierce gaze on Ivo. "And how did it all start? With someone – older? Did someone – persuade you? A stranger?"

"Oh Father, you make it sound so creepy!" Tucking her feet under her, Nevenka twisted herself into a position on the couch that only a limber seventeen-year-old could achieve. Although she was more pretty than plain, her bulky clothes and clunky glasses did their best to disguise this.

"What about you, Nevenka?" her father asked. "Did you know?"

Nevenka made a gesture of blasé dismissal. "Of course. Really, it isn't that big a deal for people of my generation."

"I knew, too," Vuksa put in, "in case anyone cares. I'd be a fool not to notice the signs, moving in artistic circles as I do."

Davor folded his arms as if seeing, at last, the complete picture. "So everyone in the family knew except me. I wasn't as perceptive as my wife, or as youthful in outlook as my daughter, or as sophisticated as my mother."

Vuksa held the glass up to the light, studying the brown liquid. "My grandfather made his own walnut brandy. He'd chop up some green walnuts and put them in a jar –"

"And you tell me now, Ivo, the day before the emergency meeting at the Ministry of Finance, a meeting at which the fate of our country, not to mention my own career, may well be decided?"

Ivo leaned forward. In appearance a younger, leaner version of Davor, Ivo had an even temper that seemed to come more from his mother. "I'm sorry, Dad, but there's another reason it just had to be today. You see, I have something else to tell you."

Davor threw up his hands. "On your first day home, you announce you're gay, you 'come out' as they say, and now you have something more to tell us?"

"My grandfather swore it had medicinal properties," Vuksa remarked. "Very good for dandruff. I must admit, I don't remember him having a speck of dandruff."

At that moment, the death rattle of the old doorbell sounded.

Davor scowled. "It's probably the widow with three cats from across the street come to tell me that she knows, too." Heaving himself up from the couch, he tried to work the intercom beside the front door, hello-ing into it to no avail. Marija reminded Davor the intercom had been broken for a week. "Oh, this miserable country!" he bellowed, slamming down the receiver. "Nothing ever works here."

"Nevenka," Marija said, "go to the street door and see who it is."

"It might be a stranger!" Nevenka wailed. "You know I hate dealing with strangers."

Sweeping her eyes over her daughter's outfit, Marija said, "Maybe it's just as well you don't go, considering how you look. You dress like you don't think anyone can see you."

"I don't care how I look. I just want to do the minimum that's necessary for me to get through another horrible day in my horrible life, then crawl under the covers."

The doorbell rang again, and Ivo moved toward the door. "I'd better go. It's probably my friend."

"Friend?" Davor barked. "What friend?"

Ivo pinched his lips together nervously. "Someone I met at my school in the U.S. He flew over with me. I told him to wait a while before he came here. I wanted to have a chance to talk to all of you before you met him."

In a quick change of mood, Nevenka's face lit up. "Ivo, is he your boyfriend? Is that the other thing you have to tell us, that you've brought your American boyfriend home with you?"

"Well, yes," Ivo stammered. "His name is Cliff, Clifford Tillman. I'm sure you'll like him."

Ivo might have been sure; the others appeared less so. A few minutes later, he ushered in a tall American of about the same age. The family fixed him with a long, dubious stare. Cliff wore jeans that said, "Casual," a black blazer and maroon shirt that said, "Yet stylish." His light brown hair was mussed in a way the family was conscious enough of Western fashions to realize was intentional.

Zablvacians had two traditional attitudes toward strangers that showed themselves at different times and in different circumstances: hospitality and hostility. Davor tried to keep in mind the former. "It's nice to meet you, Cliff," he said, offering his hand.

Cliff returned, "*Drago mi je.*" This meant "It's nice to meet you" in Zablvacian. The family looked surprised at his using their language, which few foreigners spoke. "Sorry," Cliff said, "that's about all I can say in your lingo. I hope I can pick up more during my visit."

Davor eyed the large electric-blue suitcase Cliff had brought with him. "Your visit, yes. And exactly how long will that be?"

"Can't say. I've polished off my degree in theater arts, so I'm free as a bird."

"'Free as a bird.' How nice for you."

"Super place you've got here!" Cliff exclaimed, looking around. This praise was another surprise, for the flat was small and jammed to the bursting point. Among the many objects it contained were a number of musical instruments. Vuksa had insisted her son and grandchildren learn to play at least one, though only Nevenka had shown real aptitude, on the violin.

Marija suggested they all sit down. "We hope you'll enjoy your stay here," she said to Cliff. "Our country can be rather boring for outsiders."

"Zablvacia is hard for people to get to," Vuksa observed, "and when they arrive, they wonder why they bothered."

"We don't have a beautiful coastline like Croatia," Nevenka said, "or ruins like Greece, or even Count Dracula's castle like Romania."

"From what I've seen so far, Zablvacia is totally cool," Cliff enthused. "I come from a berg in California that's proud of having a building from 1885, so a place like this just bowls me over. It's obviously had a real long history."

Vuksa gazed before her with an abstracted look. "Yes, a long history, like a long night in which you lurch from one nightmare to the next. Our country has been shrunk, expanded, swallowed whole. Decimated by floods and droughts, plague and famine. Ground under the heel of Turks, Hungarians, Serbs, and Nazis."

"Sometimes I'm not even sure Zablvacia exists," Nevenka mused. "I joined a pen pal club and wrote to a girl in Chile, and she wrote back that none of her friends had ever heard of such a place, that I must be making it up."

Several anxieties, combining forces, brought Davor to his feet. "Cliff, I hope you'll excuse me, but I must go to the office. I have an extremely important meeting tomorrow –"

Marija pointed at the portfolio Davor grabbed as he moved toward the door. "Davor, that's Nevenka's. Can't you see where she scratched it when she fell off her bike?" Davor peered at its leather sides, while Marija turned to Cliff. "I thought it was a sweet idea to give them the same portfolios at Christmas, but they're always mixing them up." Then to her daughter. "Nevenka, I've asked you to keep yours in your room."

"But it's so crowded in there with me and Gran," she said.

Rising, Marija spoke in a tone that brooked no argument. "Davor, you are going out, but not to the Ministry. This is Ivo's first day home, and Cliff's first day in our country, and the first nice day we've had for ages, and we're all going on a bike ride."

Davor let out a sigh of resignation, his big shoulders drooping.

The family packed a lunch, borrowed a neighbor's bike for Cliff, and off they went. Ivo and Cliff rode in front. Cliff gawked as he pedaled, his head swinging from side to side.

"This place is totally awesome, man! Everything is so frigging old. Of course a bunch of little things need to be tweaked. Those graffiti tags have got to go." He waved his hand at a stone facade scrawled over with purple spray paint. "The frilly frothy Franz Joseph era buildings – don't change a thing. But oh my God, those Tito era window displays! Some smart queen needs to do a complete overhaul there."

In one shop window they passed, cheap clothes drooped on hangers, squares of paper with handwritten prices pinned to them. In another, a jumble of toys, cosmetics, and cleaning products were heaped unceremoniously against the glass.

"What's the Zablvacian word for 'pizzazz'?" Cliff called out.

"I don't think there is one," Ivo returned.

"Figures."

They skimmed past a waterless fountain. "Hey, why isn't that fountain running?" Cliff asked.

"I've no idea," Ivo replied.

"Couldn't your dad find out? He works for the government, after all."

"Sure, he could talk to twenty of his colleagues. And you know what he'd get? Eleven implausible explanations, five shoulder shrugs, and four finger wags meaning, 'It's better not to ask.' Cliff, you do realize Zablvacia isn't a set in a play you're writing. It's a real country. People work here, raise children."

"Sorry, Ivo baby. You know me, reality sometimes slips my mind."

Davor and Marija rode a ways behind the two young men. Marija's long black hair was lifted by the wind, her full lips parted. Now and then, Davor thought about kissing her, and he might have found an opportunity to do this if most of his attention hadn't been focused on another matter. Not his son; that was purely a family concern. Skimming through the streets of the beloved capital of his beloved country, scattering its pigeons, bumpty-bumping over its cobblestones, Davor's mind was fixed on a much larger question. What in the world was Zablvacia going to do about those damned World Bank loans?

As they glided through Pupina Square, Davor's gaze clung to the tower of the Town Hall. Before World War II, the elaborate clock near its top had been one of the few sights that brought visitors to Zablvacia. Alas, before beating a hasty retreat toward the fatherland, the Germans had turned their machine guns on it for a few destructive minutes. After the war, the clock had been rebuilt, only now instead of statues of a knight and a woodsman and a fair maiden trundling out every hour, a soldier with a bayonet appeared, a scientist holding a test tube, a workman carrying a hammer, all stock figures from the communist pantheon.

Zablvacia did indeed possess a long, tumultuous history, as his mother had said. The string of recent upheavals flashed through Davor's mind. The war over, Tito had welded together the Federal People's Republic of Yugoslavia out of the Balkan fragments, including Zablvacia, by far the smallest. Forty years later, these burst apart again. When countries like Croatia and Slovenia declared their independence, scarcely noticed, little Zablvacia joined the rush, crying, "Me, too!" Soon war swept over much of the land once more, while the West mainly just fretted on the sidelines.

When at last the conflict ended, the West, having done little to achieve peace, tried to bring some prosperity. That was when the loans began, those wonderful, terrible loans. As an agent of the West, the World Bank was mainly concerned with the countries in the region that still suffered or simmered, but again, Zablvacia piped up, "Me, too!" They seemed such splendid gifts, those loans. Yet they proved to be pretty ribbon-tied boxes that each contained a ticking time bomb, and the hour of detonation was at hand.

Davor had seen all the communiques back and forth, including the last from the Ministry – "Revenues down, expenditures up, so sorry, emergency meeting, highest priority" – and the World Bank's response – "Pay up now or we'll make your name mud in the international credit market" (here he was paraphrasing slightly). With Head Minister Petrak issuing a plea for bold new plans to raise funds, in a rare moment of daring, Davor had been one of only two ministers to step forward.

Marija, watching her husband's gaze linger on the Town Hall, seemed to guess what he was thinking. "Is the situation really so bad, Davor? Suppose we don't repay the loans, what can the World Bank do? Foreclose on our country and make us leave?"

A dark look spread over Davor's face. "Those foreign bureaucrats will squeeze us in a thousand ways and meddle in a thousand more. The minister who saves us from this fate will earn the gratitude of the entire nation."

Davor and Marija caught up with Ivo and Cliff, who had stopped at the other side of the square. The two young men heard Davor's last words.

"We'll erect a statue of you in front of the Town Hall," Ivo teased.

Nevenka and Vuksa joined the others. "Father riding a horse!" Nevenka cried.

Vuksa sniffed. "My son has never ridden a horse in his life. I see him on a bicycle, a gleaming bronze bicycle."

"A country that's so poor one of its ministers has to ride a bicycle can't afford a statue of any kind," Marija pointed out.

The family cycled along the River Tav, which ran through the center of the city. Soon they were slipping through a narrow archway in the town walls while the river flowed through a wider opening of its own. From there, they followed the Tav on a dusty country road. Except for Cliff, they all knew where they were heading. With no need for discussion, they got off their bikes at one point and walked them along a path through the leafless woods. Here, the beauty of the day penetrated even Davor's brooding. Trees that wouldn't have merited a second glance in winter, mingling with their mundane neighbors, had transformed themselves into clouds of white or pink blossom. Birds cheeped, whistled, trilled. The crows, caught in the spring-time spell, tempered their cries to sound more like *haw* than *caw*: *haw, haw, haw*.

Coming up beside his father, Ivo asked to hear about the plan he would unveil at the meeting tomorrow. Davor knew his fellow ministers saw him as industrious, but plodding. In his son's eyes, by contrast, he was the brightest star in the Ministry firmament. No one was more likely than Ivo to tell him that, after putting his mind under tremendous pressure, he'd produced a sparkling diamond of an idea.

"What do these countries have in common?" Davor began by asking. "Monaco, Andorra, Lichtenstein, San Marino."

"They're all small," Ivo said.

"Correct. Small and stinking rich. And what's a major source of their income? Tourism, of course. People love to visit quaint little European countries. They think they're like something out of a fairy tale. Cozy, like a snug pair of slippers."

Ivo's eyes gleamed. "So why shouldn't they visit *us?*"

"Precisely. My new tourism campaign is based on the slogan" – Davor paused for effect, since he was especially proud of this –"'Narrow your horizons, come to Zablvacia.'"

"That's a great idea."

"It rocks, man," said Cliff, who had moved closer.

Davor assumed this was a compliment.

Vuksa, too, had overheard. "Not another scheme to attract tourists!" she moaned. "Haven't you learned your lesson by now, Davor? First came the Zablvacian International Film Festival, which you couldn't even get Hungarians from sixty kilometers away to attend."

"I admit –"

"Then the nudist camp you organized during the coldest, rainiest summer in our history."

Davor's small mouth tightened into a frown, as it had all his life in the face of his mother's criticisms. "But tourism is the key, I'm sure."

"Dad, can I sit in on the meeting tomorrow?" Ivo asked.

"Strictly speaking, it's not open to the public, but I'm sure no one would object."

Marija explained to Cliff, "Ivo is practically an honorary minister. Everyone assumes he'll follow in his father's footsteps. That is still your plan, isn't it, Ivo?"

"Like father, like son," Ivo smiled.

Yesterday this remark would have pleased Davor. Today his tone was ambiguous as he echoed, "Yes. Like father, like son."

Cliff clapped his hand on Davor's broad back. "Hey, can you smuggle me into this meeting, too? I'd love to get the inside scoop on how things work around here."

Davor's brown eyes widened with surprise and resistance. "Oh, well, that might be tricky. You're a foreigner, after all."

"At least we can try," Ivo said. "The worst that can happen is they'll ask Cliff to leave."

"All right," Davor said, not knowing how else to respond. "Meet me at the Town Hall in the morning. We'll see what we can do."

The path led to what had once been Davor and Marija's favorite picnic spot when they were courting and was nowadays the family's, a triangular point of land where a small stream joined the River Tav at an angle. With water flowing on two sides, it was as if they occupied the prow of a ship. Davor and Marija munched on sandwiches, sitting back to back. Vuksa sipped something out of a plastic cup – fruit juice, everyone hoped. Ivo and Cliff kept a few tactful inches of space between them. Nevenka, who had brought her sketchbook along in her portfolio, tried to capture the whole scene with her pencil.

"I want to show you my scrapbook of places I visited in the U.S.," Ivo said to Davor. He pulled the book out of his backpack and handed it to his father.

Nevenka's pencil came to a stop. "Ivo, don't move around. You're ruining my extended family portrait."

Davor turned the pages. "Key West, Fire Island, Provincetown. Very nice."

"Look, Dad, here's a map of Palm Springs. Cliff and I were there just last month."

Davor studied the gaudy sheet. "What kind of a map is this? 'Gay Hot Spots of Palm Springs,'" he read. "'Rainbow Retreat. Enjoy the sweet life at this clothing-optional men's resort. . . . Toucans Tiki Lounge, a Hawaiian dance and cruise bar.'" He frowned. "Did you like this Palm Springs, Ivo?"

"It's a fascinating place, Dad."

Cliff stretched his arms lazily, drawing a sound of annoyance from Nevenka at this further disruption. Then with a look of sudden inspiration, she turned over a page and started a new drawing.

"Palm Springs is a drag," Cliff declared. "Nothing to do but shop and look at mid-censh, mid-interesting architecture."

"In just fifteen years," Ivo said, "Palm Springs has transformed itself from a sleepy retirement community into a major gay tourist destination."

"Really?" Davor said without interest.

"Gay tourism is big business. An article I read estimated that gay people travel twenty percent more than straight ones."

This at least was pleasing to Davor. "Ah, you're quoting statistics like a true economist."

Marija looked over Nevenka's shoulder. "What are you drawing now?" she asked.

"I'm making Cliff a map of Zablvacia showing all the gay hot spots so he won't be bored."

"But we don't have any." Marija turned to her son. "Do we, Ivo?"

Ivo moved over to his sister and pointed to a spot on the map she was quickly sketching. "Put in Sumica on this corner, 'a sexy sizzling gay bar.'"

Vuksa took another sip from her cup. "Sumica isn't a gay bar. I should know, I've been singing there since my dismissal last year from the Zablvacian National Opera – a dismissal that I assure you, young man, was as unexpected as it was unjustified," she interjected to Cliff. "Sumica is a proletariat dive full of workers from the Pluzinova Cookie Factory getting drunk after a long day making second-rate cookies."

Ivo laughed. "If we put it on the map and say it's a gay bar, and the taxi drivers and hotel clerks tell people it's a gay bar, soon it will be a gay bar." He indicated another spot. "Don't forget the Superba Baths."

"Ivo," his mother protested, "that's full of old men who only want relief from their arthritis."

"I'll add more gay things," Nevenka said, "restaurants and hotels and clothing stores along Svetorgska Street."

"What else?" Ivo mused. "A hair salon. . . a disco. . . a gym."

After a few more minutes of work, Nevenka tore out the sheet and held it up for everyone to see. "Voila, a gay map of Zablvacia!"

Davor didn't even glance at the map, his thoughts straying. Had he been a fool to agree to speak at the meeting tomorrow? "Narrow your horizons" – would that slogan actually bring his fellow ministers to their feet in a storm of applause? A childhood memory circled through his mind. In a moment of un-communistic entrepreneurial zeal, he'd gotten permission from his father to sell flowers from the family's garden. He'd stood in front of their house holding out his splendid bouquets to everyone who passed, calling, "Flowers for sale! Who'll buy my beautiful flowers?" The answer: no one. Not the old woman teetering past with her wicker shopping basket. Not the man on the battered bicycle, cigarette dangling from his lips.

Davor looked at the river. After passing over or around each obstruction of rock and log, the water smoothed itself out again almost at once. Slipping onto his back and closing his eyes, Davor tried to smooth out his mind in the same way. The warmth of the day put its arms around him like a lover. Then something tickled his ear. He opened his eyes to find Marija leaning over him, playfully wielding a grass blade. Bending closer still, she whispered,

"Let's go for a little walk. Just you and I."

Davor rose, and they walked arm in arm beside the stream.

"Davor, do you remember another day in spring when we came to this spot?" Marija asked.

Davor smiled. "Of course. The day I asked you to marry me. My plan was to take you to the end of the point where the stream enters. Two ducks were already sitting there, unfortunately, a drake and a female. I didn't want to disturb them in case the drake was making his proposal, too. I had to ask my own question farther down the bank."

Although Davor had told this story many times before, he enjoyed telling it again.

"You turn some pages in the book," Marija said, "and here we are, with a daughter and a son."

Davor's mouth twitched. "And a son-in-law besides."

"An American son-in-law. He is speaking English, isn't he?"

"An American son-in-law sleeping with Ivo in our living room."

"Where else would he sleep? That's always doubled as Ivo's room."

"On our couch potato."

"Sofa-bed, darling."

"You don't suppose they'll –"

"Careful, Davor," Marija said, steering her husband around a muddy patch.

"It's not that I'm homophonic."

"Homophobic, dearest."

"My political attitudes are progressive."

As so often, Marija could guess his thoughts. "Still, it's one thing to have gay people be out there somewhere in the distance, and another to have one turn up in your own family."

"Yes," Davor admitted. After a moment, he went on, "Do you know what bothers me the most? That if Ivo is gay, that's one way he isn't like me. You know how it's been. I modeled myself on my father, and why not, he was a fine man. And Ivo did the same with me."

Marija gave a reminiscent smile. "When he was a little boy, he always wanted to go to the Ministry with you and sit at your desk."

"Ivo went to the same university I did, he studied economics, as I had. Then he won that scholarship in the United States and spent his final year there – and already that was different, not something I'd done. He didn't come home when the school year ended. He wanted to travel for another year, to discover the world, he said. And now he comes back and tells us he's gay, and again I see him move further down another path."

"You two still have a strong bond, Davor. I've envied it at times."

"I know Ivo. He'll want to learn all about gay this and gay that, history, politics, economics. And he'll want me to learn all about it, too. The idea exhausts me."

Marija stopped and faced Davor, placing her hands on the big slopes of his shoulders. "Are you too tired to give me one small kiss?"

Davor looked into Marija's eyes, which were a feline green, then lowered his gaze to the gold heart she wore on a chain around her neck. She hadn't cared about an engagement ring, and he'd given her this instead. "I give you my heart," he'd told her. He liked to see it resting there on her smooth skin, several inches above her breasts, his heart near hers.

"I'm never too tired for that." Davor kissed her once on the mouth. "That was for you." Then again. "That was for me."

Chapter 2

Davor was the first to leave the flat the next day. Without turning on a light in the living room, he crept out the door on tiptoe. He didn't want to disturb the two sleeping figures on the fold-out bed, still less to be disturbed himself by seeing them as they lay together. Soon he was getting off his bicycle before the Town Hall and hurrying up the steps, eager to take a last look at the material he'd prepared for the meeting that morning. Regrettably, he never had a chance.

The Town Hall had gone through many changes over time. During Zablvacia's early years as a separate kingdom, it served as the royal palace; later, when the kingdom was reduced to a province, as a town hall. Ten years ago when Zablvacia gained its independence, it was grandly renamed the Congress Building. This was a title no one used, for Zablvacians, so often subjected to sweeping change, resisted minor ones whenever possible.

The Town Hall was home to an ever-increasing number of bureaucrats, including several whose sole job was to reduce bureaucracy. Sixteen Ministers of Finance were jammed into the former Mayor's Robing Room. Today, with everyone in an uproar over the loan crisis, rushing madly about, raising their voices, banging file cabinets open and shut, Davor found he couldn't even think clearly about whether he should try to speak first at the meeting or second, let alone review such a complex proposal.

At ten, Ivo and Cliff arrived, and Davor felt obliged to give the American a quick tour. His tone was apologetic as he pointed out the room's four-hundred-year-old leaded windows, which let in drafts, and the crumbling stucco work on the walls.

"This sure isn't like any office you'd find back in the good old U.S. of A.," Cliff said. Davor cringed at this seeming slight, until he realized from Cliff's gleaming American smile that he was paying him a compliment.

Cliff was most impressed by the round fresco in the middle of the ceiling. In a flush of prosperity after the Peace of Rassasorrowitzki, King Stefan the Lame had commissioned it from Giovanni Sottobosco, the twenty-sixth most famous painter of his day. It was supposed to show the king as Jupiter standing on a cloud hurling thunderbolts at his country's enemies. The flush of prosperity quickly faded, as they had a tendency to do in Zablvacia. All Sottobosco had completed by the time the money ran out was a circle of sky with cherubs looking down over a painted cornice.

"Personally, I'm glad the damned thing was never finished," Davor told Cliff, gazing upward. "I like the blue hole in the ceiling, that eternally sunny sky and the little fellows looking down. Sometimes I lean back in my chair and reach out my hand, hoping one of them will pull me up into that heavenly realm. It never happens, though. I stay down here with all my problems and all my country's problems." He sighed. "I pray that the idea I'm presenting today is a brilliant one. Something that will astonish everyone and lift me right up there."

"No one works harder than you do, Dad," Ivo said.

This produced another sigh. "That's what people always say to console someone for not having any brilliant ideas."

A voice behind Davor made him start. "*Dobar dan*, Davor."

Davor turned to face a woman of his age, with hennaed hair and a wry smile.

"*Dobar dan*, Ranka." Davor's tone was polite, but cool. "Ranka, you remember my son, Ivo."

Ranka shook his hand. "Of course. You look more like your father every time I see you, Ivo."

"Yes," Davor said, "like father, like son. And this is his –" He hesitated, embarrassed, then settled on, "his friend, his American friend, Clifford Tillman."

After turning her smile on Cliff, Ranka asked Davor if she could have a word in private. They moved over to a window.

"That's Ranka Vilović," Ivo said to Cliff in a low voice. "She and Dad have a love-hate relationship, only without the love."

"What's their problem?" Cliff asked.

"They were engaged when they were at university together, but Dad broke it off after he met my mom."

"Your dad is so square. I wouldn't have thought he'd have it in him to jilt someone."

"Too bad, he could have become a filthy capitalist. When the Pluzinova Cookie Factory was privatized, Ranka's family bought it for a song."

"Shh, I'm trying to hear what they're saying."

With Davor raising his voice, they caught, "For the last time, no! And again no. No, no, no!"

"Always no to me, Davor," Ranka said. "Why not yes for a change?"

The two ministers stalked away from each other. Davor rejoined Ivo and Cliff. "That woman infuriates me!" he cried.

"She begged me to abandon whatever proposal I was going to make and throw all my support behind hers. The nerve! Well, I'll show her."

Snatching up his portfolio, Davor marched ahead of them down the hall to the Grand Salon. This was hung with tapestries faded to a pleasant blur and lit by several dusty crystal chandeliers. Davor directed Ivo and Cliff to sit in the back, telling them to try to be inconspicuous. He and Ranka took their places on either side of a lectern. The other Ministers of Finance bustled in, talking excitedly, and settled in rows of chairs facing them.

Ivo slipped informational morsels to Cliff. The blustering man with a big mustache was Minister Smajlović, he told him. "Staunch Catholic, about as far to the right as he can go without falling off the scale." The doddering old man was Minister Ozbolf, "deaf as a post."

"And that's Head Minister Petrak," Ivo said as a man with hesitant step and wild gray mane entered. Petrak almost departed through the door on the far side of the room. Recollecting himself at the last minute, he took his place behind the lectern. "He's darling," Ivo whispered, "but a little absent-minded."

After a few bangs of a gavel, Petrak swept his eyes over the audience. "My fellow ministers," he began in his quavering voice, "our country faces its gravest crisis in recent years. With storm clouds overhead, we tread on thin ice toward a yawning chasm, while the sword of Damocles is poised above our Achilles heel like a snake in the grass."

After some concerned mutterings from the ministers, Petrak went on, "We must find a new source of revenue to repay our loans to the World Bank. This task has to engage our complete attention. Our gaze must never waver from it for an instant."

Breaking off, Petrak lifted a hand to one ear. "Ah, I can hear the swallows chirping away under the Town Hall eaves – delightful! Their merry song assures us that spring has indeed arrived at last. 'Spring hopes eternal,' as they say. Nevertheless, the air is still rather chilly this morning. As I grow older, I feel the cold more. I don't know if that's everyone's experience, but it certainly is mine. In any case, I thank you."

Petrak was moving away from the lectern when Smajlović intervened. "Head Minister, I believe you have more to say."

Petrak knitted his thick white brows. "Do I? Oh yes, of course." He returned to his post. "Two ministers have answered my plea for proposals. We'll hear first from Ranka Vilović. She's one of our brightest lights, a minister who combines creativity with pragmatism and self-confidence with humility."

Ranka took Petrak's place behind the lectern. "Fellow ministers," she declared, "Zablvacia is a small, insignificant place. We've brought forth no great artists, thinkers, religious or military leaders. We can't compete with other countries in the production of a single item. Very well then, I say we should make the most of our mediocrity."

Ranka motioned to an assistant in the doorway, who trundled in a wheeled table holding a sleek laptop and video screen.

Davor's eyes grew wide at the sight. How had Ranka persuaded Petrak to pay for such luxuries when, as Cliff had pointed out, the other equipment in the Ministry belonged in a museum of information technology? Then it came to him – she'd bought them herself, out of the Pluzinova Cookie fortune. Davor cast an embarrassed look at the rickety wooden easel beside him that he planned to use in his own presentation.

With the click of a mouse, Ranka called up an image on the screen. This was a variation on the famous depiction of man evolving from apes, only here it was a more recent development that was shown. A classic hominid was succeeded by five versions of himself growing progressively plumper.

"The average American is ten percent fatter than he was a decade ago," Ranka said, "and Europeans are getting more rotund, too. This has resulted in a huge market for low fat and non-fat foods. We in Zablvacia can tap into that."

Restless, Davor opened his portfolio in preparation for his turn and removed the papers inside. A look of horror came over his face when, instead of the expected charts and diagrams, he found a stack of watercolors and pencil drawings. He'd taken the wrong portfolio when he left the flat that morning! Hadn't he placed his to the right of the front door before he went to bed? Or was it to the left?

With another click from Ranka, a box of cookies appeared on the screen. Against a poisonous yellow background, PLUZ-INOVA COOKIES was written in crude block letters.

"In the waning years of Yugoslavia, President Tito graciously bestowed on Zablvacia its one and only manufacturing plant, the Pluzinova Cookie Factory. The cookies we make there are not so bad, not so good. Very well then, we'll sell them to the West, along with a whole line of other foods, under the brand name Good Enough. It doesn't matter whether these cookies are high fat or low because you won't want to eat very many."

Next, Ranka played a commercial in which a Zablvacian housewife handed a plate of cookies to her husband.

"Another cookie, dearest?" the housewife asked.

"No, thank you, my pet," the husband replied. "One was enough." The man passed the plate to his young daughter. Unenthusiastic, she took one cookie, broke it in half, and returned the other to the plate.

Gazing into the camera, the housewife urged, "Buy Good Enough Cookies for your family today. They won't want more than one or two – because they're only Good Enough."

Switching off the screen, Ranka concluded, "I urge the Ministry to accept this proposal because I firmly believe that it is – *good enough*."

The ministers chuckled at her little joke while Petrak murmured dreamily, "'They won't want more than one or two'. . . ." Recollecting himself, he rose. "Thank you Ranka Vilović for your highly interesting presentation. Next we'll hear from Davor Matošić. Davor is a minister who. . . But all the same no one can deny that he . . . Well, I'm sure we can all at least agree that Davor is very hard-working."

Although Petrak made a gesture of invitation, Davor's heavy form remained fixed to his seat.

"Come Davor, we're eager to hear what you have to say. . . . 'They won't want more than two or three.' Very good."

At last Davor moved to the lectern, dragging the easel with him. His mouth felt dry, his forehead damp. He gazed out at the audience, searching for a friendly face. He could find only one, that of his son, who beamed encouragement at him. Perhaps two, if he included Cliff, whose gaze at least suggested that he was curious and open-minded.

Davor cleared his throat. "Ladies and gentlemen, my proposal can be summed up in one word. . . . Yes, just one word. . . Only one . . . little . . . word."

The ministers grew restless, shifting in their chairs. Desperate, Davor shuffled through Nevenka's sheets, looking for anything remotely useful. A pot of geraniums? No. A beetle, lace curtains lifting in a breeze, an old man hoeing in a garden? No, no, no. Suddenly, one drawing did rivet his attention. He glanced at Ivo and Cliff.

"My proposal can be summed up in two words, actually. The first will come as no surprise. That word is Tourism."

The ministers set up a muttering that communicated, We've heard this before.

At that moment, Nevenka rushed into the room gripping her father's portfolio. A gesture from Davor kept her from approaching. Ivo waved Nevenka over, and she sat beside him. Her face was red both from her furious bicycle ride after discovering the mix-up and this unwelcome public exposure.

Squaring his large shoulders, Davor had the air of someone taking the plunge. "The other word no doubt will come as a surprise. That word is – gay. *Homoseksualac.*" He slapped Nevenka's Gay Hot Spots Map onto the easel. "Gay tourism!"

Kaleidoscopic reactions from the ministers, of indignation, amusement, disbelief. Looks of amazement from Nevenka, Ivo, and Cliff.

Davor's mind was like a machine getting up to speed, whirring and clanking. "Gay tourism is big business, but if most of us think about it at all, we think, Oh yes, gay people go to large cities like Berlin and Amsterdam, resorts like Sitges, Mykonos. I say, why shouldn't they come to Zablvacia? Why not turn our country into the newest gay Mecca? As a first step, I urge that we change our country's name."

Minister Smajlović jumped to his feet. "Change our name? You can't be serious."

"Let Davor speak," Petrak insisted. "We're only at the stage of words, and words do no harm." His eyes wandered. "Though in fact that may not be entirely true. 'In the beginning of all mischief was the Word. . .'"

Davor rushed on. "Zablvacia has been known by a dozen names during its long history. In the fourteen hundreds, in the rein of Orseg the Civil, it was the Kingdom of Gaidonika. I propose we revive this name in slightly altered form as 'Gaydonia.'" He scrawled across the map below "Gay Hot Spots" the words "Of Gaydonia."

Ranka gave a toss of her hennaed head. "Davor, you want us to fling open our doors to the gays? That really is too much."

Minister Ozbolf leaned forward, cupping one hand beside his better ear. "Davor wants us to take in the strays? How would it help to have lots of dogs and cats running around?"

"Even assuming we'd accept the presence of such visitors," Smajlović cried, "how could your plan succeed? What do you intend to offer them?"

"We'll give them not just a gay neighborhood, not even a city, but an entire gay country."

"But gay people must want to visit places where there are others like them," Ranka said, "and there are hardly any here in Zablvacia."

Davor asserted, "The secret of success will be to ensure a proper mass."

"Davor wants us to say a proper mass for the poor animals?" Ozbolf questioned, perplexed. "That would be most unorthodox. 'Pussy cat of God, who taketh away the sins of the world, have mercy upon us.'"

"This brings me to my next proposal. And that is. . ." Davor riffled through Nevenka's pictures. A watercolor of a chestnut tree in bloom caught his eye, and he placed this on the easel. "And that involves our annual Chestnut Blossom Festival in May."

Smajlović writhed in his seat. "The idea of using the Chestnut Blossom Festival to attract a bunch of sissified gadabouts – why, it's sacrilege! The festival commemorates a sacred event, a woodcutter's vision of the Virgin Mary seated atop a chestnut tree wearing a wreath of its snowy white blossoms."

"In truth, the festival's origins go back to pagan fertility rites," Davor countered, "so we needn't be too fussy. We emphasize that the wreaths the women wear in the procession represent –" As bold as Davor had been so far, at this point prudery overcame him, and the most he could do was form a circle with his hands. "And that the poles carried by the men –" He delineated a long erect object. "Well, I'm sure you get the idea. We'll deluge the gay media with spicy ads for the Festival and pray that people come."

"The price is too high," Smajlović stormed, "to have such people in our midst. I'm sure Minister Ozbolf is of the same mind."

Ozbolf nodded vigorously. "Our own kind – yes, I agree our first priority is to them. This country must not be made a refuge for every footloose feline and carefree canine that comes along."

Petrak smiled, lost in his own world. "'We don't want more than five or six. . . .'"

Davor took another plunge. "You have at least one gay person in your midst right now, and I doubt he's done you any harm. I'd like to present my son, Ivo Matošić."

Ivo stood up hesitantly. The ministers gasped with surprise.

Davor opened his arms in a concluding gesture he remembered from a rhetoric class at university. "My fellow ministers, think of how we've been characterized by the rest of the world, as barbarians, those crazy Balkans. Which would you prefer, to be known as the Powder Keg of Europe – or the Powder Puff?"

The ministers leaped collectively to their feet, arguing among themselves, while Petrak made vain attempts to calm them. In the midst of all this commotion, Davor sent Ivo a quiet father-to-son look that said, "I gave it my best shot."

Chapter 3

"You've done what?" Vuksa demanded of Davor. "You proposed turning Zablvacia into *Gaydonia*?"

Vuksa had just joined the family and Cliff that evening in the office of Head Minister Petrak, where they'd been summoned by his secretary. A map of the Balkans hung behind an antique desk stained so dark a brown that it looked like an immense bar of chocolate.

Vuksa turned to Cliff and Ivo. "Please understand that I have nothing against you darling gay people. Not as long as you stay in your place, which is out in the seats of a theater where I'm performing or helping backstage." Then to Davor, "And why in heaven's name has the Head Minister gathered the entire family here? Are we being deported on charges of sheer idiocy thanks to your mad scheme?"

"I've no idea, mother," Davor said. "We'll have to wait and see."

"Davor, man," Cliff said, "do you really want hordes of gay tourists traipsing through your quiet streets?"

"We aren't figments out of some dusty old European farce you're directing," Ivo said to him impatiently. "We have to put food on the table and clothes on our backs, and maybe this plan would do that."

Davor was silent, his bulky, dark-suited figure pacing up and down.

"You worry me when you're quiet," Marija said. "Tell me what you're thinking."

"I'm thinking about English grammar," Davor replied.

Marija looked puzzled. "English grammar?"

"I was reviewing it the other day, the part about Comparisons and the Superlative. I know I'm *smart*, and I know I'm *smarter* than many people, but the *smartest*, that's something I've never been. For once in my life, I want to be the smartest. I thought Gaydonia might be the way."

"Your family loves and admires you, Davor. Doesn't that count for something?"

"Yes, but I want more. I want my neighbors to love and admire me, the old woman selling apples in Pupina Square, the whole country. Does that seem foolish?"

Marija held his hand for a moment. "Perhaps, but in a very sweet way."

The door creaked open, and Petrak wandered in. "This is a pleasant surprise!" he exclaimed. He shook hands with Marija, who was closest to the desk and its two lamps, which were the only source of illumination. "Dr. Matošić, a pleasure as always. How are things faring in the Ministry of Health?"

In a poor country like Zablvacia, Marija only managed to have a few private patients, with most of her time taken up by a job at the Ministry of Health. "The drug addicts haven't given me much trouble lately, Head Minister, but the wife beaters are quite a handful."

"Indeed, indeed. And Ivo!" Petrak said, catching sight of him. "Welcome back from your studies abroad. Did you enjoy Caledonia?"

"It was California, Head Minister," Ivo said.

"Yes, of course. I'm always mixing up the two. My great-aunt's husband was a Scotsman, you see. I'm afraid it was not a happy marriage."

Davor brought Nevenka forward into the light. "My daughter, Nevenka."

"Delighted."

"And I don't believe you've met my mother, Vuksa Ćuruvija."

Petrak's eyes grew large and round at this name, and his wild white hair seemed to quiver with excitement. "Not Vuksa Ćuruvija, the famous singer!" he cried as she stepped toward him. "Why, Davor, I had no idea she was your mother." He kissed Vuksa's hand. One had the impression he might even have knelt before her if the shakiness of his limbs hadn't advised against this.

"I'm a huge fan of yours, Madam Ćuruvija," Petrak gushed. "I saw every one of your performances in *The Serpent Bridegroom*. Let me see, how many years ago was that?"

To spare him the trouble of tedious calculations, Vuksa hurried in with, "It was among the high points of my career."

A look of shyness came into Petrak's face. "Do you remember how a secret admirer would send you a bunch of violets every evening? That was me, back when I was an impetuous young bachelor."

"How extraordinary!"

"You turned my head and swept me off my feet and set my heart on fire."

Vuksa let loose an attractive, though somewhat theatrically practiced laugh. "That all sounds quite painful."

Last, Davor presented Cliff, who by this point had achieved the status of "Ivo's American boyfriend." The introductions over, there was a silence while Petrak lifted some of the papers on his desk, peering at them through reading glasses.

"Head Minister," Davor prompted, "you asked us all to come here."

"Ah yes, of course!" Petrak exclaimed. "Well, Davor, after much consideration, I've decided to adopt your proposal."

"Head Minister Petrak, I'm honored, I'm overwhelmed, I —"

"I'm placing the entire staff of the Ministry of Finance at your disposal."

"I don't know how to thank you."

"We'll see if you're still thanking me a month from now. I must warn you, your plan will face intense opposition."

Nevenka shrank into herself like a sensitive plant someone had brushed against. "Father, will people spit on us in the street?" Davor patted her arm reassuringly.

"That's why I'm enlisting the help of your family," Petrak said. "If you can find support anywhere, it should be in your inner circle." His attention was drawn back to the irresistible magnet. "Madam Ćuruvija, your pianissimi were spun sugar, your legato melted butter. Your cry when the bridegroom enters the bedchamber on your wedding night and you discover his true nature, the mixture of horror and fascination you conveyed — it makes me shiver just to think of it."

Vuksa gave a smile made rather jagged by her poorly executed lipstick. "It was amazing what life I could breathe into that claptrap. I learned to be wary of composers whose musical education came entirely from their work as church bell ringers."

Davor took a step toward Petrak. "I don't understand what you mean, Head Minister. About enlisting the help of my family."

Petrak explained. Marija was to manage the psychological aspects of the project. Nevenka, "the Rembrandt of Cartography," was to refine her map and help prepare other publicity materials – a role Nevenka accepted on condition she didn't have to talk to a lot of people. Drawing on his time abroad, Ivo would act as an expert on gay culture in the West.

"Cliff can help, too," Ivo said. "He's a real Westerner."

"I don't know, Ivo," Cliff said doubtfully. "I came to Zablvacia for quaintness, not queerness."

"Any assistance you can give us will be greatly appreciated," Petrak said. Then to Vuksa, "Please tell me where you're performing now, Madam Ćuruvija. I'd love to hear you sing again."

"At Sumica, that wonderfully unpretentious bar by the train station. The workers from the cookie factory adore me."

Petrak raised an index finger sagely. "Culture shouldn't be the preserve of an elite. That's one of the lessons of communism we should still keep in mind."

The meeting apparently over, the family moved toward the door, until Petrak spoke again.

"Did I say the entire staff would be at your disposal, Davor? Actually, only half. Because I've also approved Ranka Vilović's plan."

"What?" Davor almost shouted.

"I found it difficult to choose between homosexuals and inferior baked goods."

"But –"

"Selecting both plans was in keeping with our national tradition of indecision. It was indecision that kept us out of the recent conflicts in our region, after all." Petrak turned his gaze to the map behind the desk. "Time and again, we told the warring factions we were just on the point of siding with them, so would they please not invade us quite yet."

Davor took up the thread. "And by the time the fighting was over, we were still just on the point of taking sides."

"Precisely. So we'll have a contest. The scheme that first brings in five million Zablvacian kunars will become official government policy. The other will be dropped, though in our country, one can never be entirely sure. Well, thank you all for coming."

Another move toward the door, halted by another remark. "Oh, one more thing. The funds I've allocated to the plans are very small. That's one of the appealing points of both, that we can implement them cheaply. Good evening."

The family surged out of the room, Davor leading the way. "I'll never pull this off!" he cried. "I haven't the faintest notion where to begin."

They plunged down the central marble staircase. This ran through several floors in the open foyer of the Town Hall, dividing into two sections between each floor before coming together again. Davor and Ivo took one side, the rest of the family the other.

"Dad, you've already had some amazing ideas," Ivo said, "and you'll have more if you just give yourself the chance. The whole family is behind you."

Near the balustrade, shallow dips had been worn into the steps by centuries of use. Vuksa, a little breathless, pitched dangerously to and fro on her high heels. "The whole family is not behind you, Davor," she insisted. "I told you, I think this is a terrible plan. But you didn't listen to me when you were a boy, and you still don't now that you're a man."

"All those strangers coming here!" Nevenka fretted.

"How will such a drastic change affect the psychological well-being of our community?" Marija pondered.

Davor came to a sudden halt mid-floor. "Maybe it is a terrible plan. Hordes of tourists. *Gay* tourists. Social unrest."

"Dad, it's a great plan," Ivo assured him. "It's – the smartest."

Davor took hold of Ivo's shoulders. "Do you really think so, Ivo?"

"Yes, and I can tell you the first thing we need to do: get all the local gay people involved."

"Of course!" Davor called over to Marija on the other side of the staircase. "Marija, do we know any gay people?"

"I have my suspicions about a colleague at the Ministry of Health," she replied. "Every August for the past fifteen years, she's gone on holiday with the same 'woman friend.'"

"You must ask her to help us. Tell her momentous changes are about to take place in Zablvacia."

A harrumph from Vuksa. "Tell her she'll wake up one day to find she doesn't even live in Zablvacia anymore, but Gaydonia."

Cliff made a face. "'Gaydonia' – yuckia!"

Davor bit the knuckle of a thumb, a habit of his when thinking hard. "But we need more such people. I have it!" Whipping out his mobile, he dialed a number. "Tomislav, it's your old school cum Davor Matošić. How are you? . . . I'm fine, and I'll be especially fine if you'll agree to do me a favor. . . . No, I don't need anyone tailed, wire-tapped, or thrown in jail. Now listen. . ."

Chapter 4

Two days later, Davor and Ivo stood at the front of the Grand Salon beside a stalwart man in a police uniform. Before them was seated a group of men and women. At first glance, it was difficult to tell what they had in common. At second and third glance as well, for that matter. Davor thanked everyone for coming. When he mentioned that some people had been invited by Sergeant Janković, a bearded man in the audience leaped to his feet.

"Sergeant Janković," he said, "has the government reinstated Article 186 of the Yugoslav Penal Code? Is this one of your round-ups, like in the old days?"

Janković rocked slightly forward and back as he stood, his hands behind him. "It was necessary for me to be the one to contact some of you. I handled your cases when our country was part of Yugoslavia, so there could be no question of a breach of privacy. I remember you, and you remember me."

"Yes, I remember you, Sergeant Janković," the bearded man said with a hostile smile. "You arrested me for soliciting sex among the underbrush in the hillier and less frequented end of Kaladin Park. You detained me at police headquarters for twenty-four hours. You told me I should have no thought in the use of my sexual organs other than producing new workers for the socialist state."

Janković continued rocking, unperturbed, "And after that, Mr. Isakov, I released you for lack of evidence, though if I recall correctly, there was in fact one very large piece."

Davor made an effort to take back the reins of the meeting. "Those of you active in gay organizations were contacted by me."

A young woman with a page-boy cut popped up. "I'm Dubravka Babović, president of Inqueerzicija. In Zablvacia, homosexuality is no longer illegal, but still frowned on. Yet you say our country is asking us to come to its aid?"

"I – that is to say we –"

With his father faltering, Ivo stepped in. "Incredible as it may seem, the answer is yes. We're being lifted out of the ash heap and invited to the ball in the castle."

A man with a shaved head consulted his notes. "You want us to help train government personnel?"

"Yes," Davor said.

"To encourage foreign friends to vacation here?"

"Yes."

"You're giving us discounts and free tickets to use with the new gay businesses and cultural attractions?"

"Yes. And we'll consider any suggestions from you about how to make this plan a success."

"What if the plan fails?" Ms. Babović asked. "Will we be blamed?"

The man with the shaved head jabbed his pen toward Davor. "What if it succeeds and people resent our newly elevated position in society?"

Davor and Ivo looked at each other, both at a loss. "Those are all. . ." Davor began.

"Excellent questions," Ivo concluded.

Later that same day, Davor and Ivo were back in the Grand Salon. Some of the gay people from that morning's meeting, including Mr. Isakov and Ms. Babović, were now stationed behind them, while before them on the much-worn parquet floor stood half the Ministers of Finance. These were mainly men in cheaply made dark suits, along with a smaller number of women wearing the female equivalents.

This was Davor's least favorite part of the plan that he and Ivo had thrown together. He'd tried to persuade Ivo to take charge of it. However, his son had insisted that he must do it. "You work with these people," he'd said. "They respect you."

Davor explained to the ministers that they'd been assigned to help implement the Gaydonia plan. "I realize you may have reservations –"

"We certainly do," Smajlović snorted.

"But I'm sure you all want to help your country in its hour of need."

Ozbolf said, "I for one refuse to lour and plead."

"I propose we entertain our new guests with Zablvacia's Scarf Dance," Davor said. "Gentlemen, please form two lines facing each other. Ladies, do the same."

The Scarf Dance was traditionally performed in same-sex groups, and Davor was glad to see the ministers went along with this idea, the men shuffling off to one side of the room, the women to the other.

"Everyone choose a partner and stand across from him or her," Davor called out. "Someone you get along with especially well, since we have many hours of rehearsal ahead of us. Your best friend – yes, choose your best friend in the Ministry."

"I suppose that's you, Ozbolf," Smajlović said, settling across from him.

"You suppose I'll do?" Ozbolf said, a little affronted. "Well, I suppose you will, too."

Mr. Isakov handed red silk scarves to one line of men and one line of women. At a signal from Davor, Ms. Babović started a CD of folk music. The ministers danced. Most of them hadn't performed the Scarf Dance since they were in school, and in spite of their qualms, they couldn't help enjoying themselves. At any rate, they seemed to feel, this was better than sitting at their desks reading someone's dull report or writing ones themselves that were even duller. They made mistakes with the steps, but this only sparked some laughter. The scarves rose and fell between the partners' hands, knees bent and straightened, shoes brushed against the floor.

"Excellent!" Davor said when the dance was finished. "Now the partner you chose for the dance will remain your partner in another endeavor. We're encouraging local gay people to make our guests feel welcome. However, their numbers are small, and you, dear ministers, must swell their ranks."

"Give them thanks?" Ozbolf cried. "Never!"

"Together with your dance partner, you'll patronize the new gay establishments. You'll mingle with our visitors and make them think they've never before met such hospitable comrades."

The ministers erupted into protest. Maybe dealing with dull reports wasn't the worst part of their job after all.

"However," Davor half-shouted over the din, "you won't be asked to do anything but talk. Our visitors will find you not only the most hospitable comrades, but the most faithful to their partners. We'll teach you how to say in a dozen languages,

'I'm very sorry, I already have a partner, and he or she is right here.'" Davor pulled Mr. Isakov toward him to illustrate.

Despite these assurances, the ministers' voices only grew louder, their gestures more emphatic. Motioning Ivo and the gay contingent toward the door, then backing in that direction himself, Davor poured out, "Thank you for coming we do appreciate it rehearsals tomorrow at nine must dash so much to do."

Chapter 5

During the next few weeks, Davor seemed to be everywhere at once in Zablvacia, usually with Ivo at his side. He'd never worked as hard in his life or enjoyed himself so much. He had a plaster cast of Michelangelo's David installed in the lobby of the Hotel Kasina, and *poof!*, it was a gay hotel. At the Zablvacian National Gallery, he brought in an artist to remove any fig leaves added to the nudes during more straitlaced times. At the country's one cinema, down came the poster for the locally made film *Boja Siva*, showing an alienated-looking couple sitting across from each other at a kitchen table, and up went a poster for *All About Eve*, with Bette Davis twirling a cocktail glass. In Kaladin Park, the pony ride was transformed into the Brokeback Mountain Experience. The bored attendant holding the ponies' reins was costumed in jeans, fringed shirt, and a cowboy hat, though even Davor couldn't keep him from still looking bored. Davor was meticulous in his attention to detail. He had Nevenka design a line of "Greetings from Gaydonia" postcards, but retained final decisions for himself and chose the shot of Ivo clad in nothing but leather chaps riding a motorcycle past the Bishop's Palace that he felt was the most aesthetically pleasing.

The bishop residing in the palace in question was a Catholic one, Bishop Zuzul. Bishop Zuzul, Bishop Kersovani from the Eastern Orthodox church, and Grand Mufti Suvar, leader of the country's Muslims, proved to be the foremost enemies of Gaydonia. During the Balkan Wars, Davor had admired the united front these three gray eminences showed in resisting the sectarian strife that afflicted Zablvacia's neighbors. He was less pleased to have them come together against his own plan. Spurred on by them, Zablvacians bombarded the government with letters condemning Gaydonia as anti-religion, anti-tradition, and just generally in poor taste. Most letters were delivered by mail, with the exception of a few that were wrapped around rocks and thrown through the windows of the Town Hall. Finally, Davor sent an urgent request to the three men, asking them to meet with him and Ivo to see if they could resolve their differences.

As the meeting got underway, Davor feared a rout. The elderly trio in their long robes marshaled an impressive array of quotations, flipping backward and forward in their holy books, stabbing the page here, there. In the case of Bishop Zuzul, it didn't help that Davor spent most Sundays watching him perform mass in St. Stephan's Cathedral. How could he argue theology and morality with someone who regularly gave him Christ's blood to drink and flesh to eat? Thankfully, just when Davor felt tempted to admit defeat, Ivo rushed into the breach.

"Gentlemen," he said, "your faiths have survived over time because of their largeness of vision. Some of the most moving stories in the Bible involve what look to modern eyes like same-sex couples. David and Jonathan, for example."

"Ah, one of my favorite passages!" Zuzul enthused, fingering his purple sash. "'The soul of Jonathan was knit with the soul of David, and Jonathan loved him as his own soul.'"

"Or Ruth and Naomi."

"Another lovely story. 'Wither thou goest, I will go; and where thou lodgest, I will lodge.'"

Ivo turned to Grand Mufti Suvar. "The Koran says that in paradise, believers will be attended by boys 'as beautiful as pearls.'"

Suvar tore through the pages of his Koran, searching for the relevant passage. "Regrettably misunderstood. . ." he muttered. "Meant only as a metaphor . . ."

Zuzul cut in with, "'Boys as beautiful as pearls.' Shame on you, Suvar, for never sharing that particular 'pearl' with me." Of the three men, Zuzul seemed the least stern in his opposition. At the same time, he dominated the talk, giving Davor the impression he enjoyed the sound of his own mellifluous voice.

Davor tried a personal appeal to Zuzul. "Bishop, you've known me all my life. Can you believe I would advocate a plan that ran contrary to the essentials of my faith?"

Zuzul smoothed out some folds in his robe with his plump, be-ringed hands. "Speaking from a personal standpoint, Davor, I might be sympathetic. After all, one never knows what circumstances may lead a convert one's way. Picture a typical gay tourist. He enters a church, inappropriately dressed, as they so often are, in short shorts and a scanty sleeveless shirt. He comes merely as a sightseer, the big telescopic lens of his camera thrusting forward. Looking around him, his interest is aroused by certain images. Christ in the Tenth Station of the Cross, his garments torn from him to reveal the splendor of his youthful form. St. Sebastian, his lithe torso pierced by a dozen arrows. Suppose I enter the scene just then. At a well-chosen word from me, overcome by a flood of strange emotions, the tourist might drop to his knees or join me in the dark confines of a confessional. . . . However, I must answer to my superiors in Rome, who tend to be less imaginative in their views."

"Is there nothing I can do to change your stand against Gaydonia?" Davor asked.

"I'm afraid not, my son."

Davor swung his heavy brown gaze toward Suvar. "Is that true for you as well?"

"Absolutely," Suvar replied.

"And you, Bishop Kersovani?"

"Positively."

Davor looked at Ivo, who gave a slight nod. It was time to roll out what they'd agreed beforehand was their one and only big gun.

"I know how much influence you three wield," Davor said. "If you're truly unswerving in your opposition to Gaydonia, my son and I might as well give up on the idea." At this, the three old men exchanged self-satisfied looks. Davor added, "Yet it does seem a pity in that case that my pie chart will come to nothing."

"What is this thing you call a 'pie chart'?" Bishop Kersovani inquired.

Davor twiddled a pen nonchalantly between two thick fingers. "Oh, it only shows how some of the projected revenues from Gaydonia will be divided among various groups. Including religious groups. I worked hard to give each of your communities a generous piece of the pie. I have the chart right here." He patted his leather portfolio, which lay beside him on the table.

All three men leaned forward. "Well, I suppose. . ." said one.

"It wouldn't do any harm. . ." added another.

"Just to take a quick look. . ." concluded the third.

With opposition from this quarter silenced, Davor focused his attention on Zablvacia's business community. Here, his task was made easier thanks to a docility left over from the communist era, when merchants were accustomed to following orders from the state, even those they considered ludicrous or objectionable. The bookshop owners dutifully placed the complete works of Oscar Wilde and Gertrude Stein in their windows, as instructed. The pharmacies stocked more than one brand of shampoo, the clothing stores other forms of underwear beside ample white boxer shorts. These were measures that Ivo assured his father would make their gay visitors feel at home.

Day by day as Davor walked the streets, they looked more like those of Gaydonia and less like those of Zablvacia. One shop, however, made itself impervious to change, and it was conspicuously placed right on Pupina Square. Davor and Ivo paid it a visit to look into the problem.

The elderly couple who owned the shop exemplified the country at its most traditional. In other words, they were grumpy and taciturn. Their shelves were stocked with only the most basic household necessities in the most bleakly packaged forms: scratchy toilet paper, dishwashing liquid of a virulent green. Davor reminded the owners they would receive a substantial tax break if they stocked nine items from the Gaydonia Catalog the Ministry had sent them. The old woman reported they were just about to put these on display. She banged onto the counter a box containing nine "Pecker Cupcake Pans."

Davor pointed at the box. "That's only one item."

"No, nine," she said. "We'll sell these disgusting things individually."

"Madam, we mean nine different items, and more than one of each."

"Nine of these," she insisted. "Nothing else."

"There's also the matter of the flag above your door," Ivo said. "We'd like you to remove your Zablvacian flag and fly one of these instead."

The shopkeeper was a woman of few words, and her husband, who hadn't yet spoken, a man of even fewer. However, the rainbow flag Ivo unfurled before them acted like a cape to a bull, and the woman made a fierce verbal charge.

"You wish me to take down the Zablvacian flag, the revered symbol of our motherland? With its red stripe standing for the blood of our martyrs, its white stripe our peaceful lamb-like nature, and blue stripe our devotion to God, and in the center a shield containing a golden goat rampant on two crossed oak branches representing our verdant forests and wearing a wreath of wheat emblematic of our agricultural bounty, and beneath the shield a banner bearing the year 681, a date carved into the mind of every Zablvacian, in which in one fell swoop Caslav Klonimir defeated the Bulgarians at the Battle of Sooty Mountain, married his only daughter Draga to the župan of Travunija, and ascended the throne as our country's first king, though whether he actually existed is admittedly a matter of scholarly debate? You wish me to replace the flag of Zablvacia with this gaudy, meretricious piece of Sodomite rubbish?"

Quailing before this onslaught, Davor took a step backward. "Yes, but only during the tourist season."

Ivo, more composed, turned to his father. "Dad, wouldn't this shop be the perfect location for the new tourist office?"

Davor's face brightened. "That's an excellent idea. We could offer the landlord a much higher rent than these people."

The old woman's grim expression turned to one of dismay. "My husband and I have run this shop for most of our lives," she wailed. "We'd be lost without it."

"That's why I'm sure you'll want to maximize your income by catering to our new guests," Davor said.

The old woman snatched the rainbow flag from Ivo as a sign of capitulation. "Next you'll ban the Zablvacian national anthem and replace it with something from – from Broadway!"

The two elderly shopkeepers hurled a defiant rendition of this anthem at Davor and Ivo as they departed.

> Our dear land,
> So gracious and so brave,
> Though you are quite small,
> It's only you we crave.
>
> River Tav,
> Please tell the world it's true,
> A Za-bl-vac-i-an,
> Loves this land bijou!

Chapter 6

No matter how much progress he made with Gaydonia, Davor never forgot that his rival, Ranka Vilović, was a force to be reckoned with. "I made the mistake of underestimating her twenty-odd years ago when I broke off our engagement," he told Ivo. "I thought she'd say, 'No worries, these things happen.' Instead, she whipped up a battle royal between us that put crows feet beside my eyes and the first gray hairs on my head."

Davor watched with trepidation as Ranka diversified the foods manufactured in the Pluzinova Factory. She soon had a ship halfway across the Atlantic jammed with Extra Mediocre Cheddar Cheese, Five Hundred Island Dressing, Neither Sweet Nor Sour Sauce, and a variety of other somewhat tantalizing products.

Ranka had immense business skills and the equally immense Pluzinova fortune at her disposal. In his darker moments, Davor would question what forces he had on his side. Certainly not all the members of his family, as Head Minister Petrak had supposed. While Ivo was in the pro-Gaydonia camp, Vuksa and Cliff were as firmly entrenched in the anti, while Marija and Nevenka wavered maddeningly between the two.

"Gaydonia has brought nothing but disruption into our lives," Vuksa asserted at a typical family dinner, brandy glass in hand. "You and Ivo always flitting off somewhere, the telephone ringing constantly."

"Davor, man," Cliff warned, "you're going to turn this into a zombie city like Prague or Dubrovnik, without an iota of real life."

Ivo rolled his eyes. "You're so sure about everything, Cliff."

"You used to like that about me, baby doll."

"Not when you're so sure about what a whole country should do. *My* country."

"The Gaydonia Hotline I set up is flooded with calls," Marija put in. "People want to know if they could be gay themselves, or their husband, mother, brother, best friend."

Nevenka bit her fingernails. "I keep having nightmares like the Sorcerer's Apprentice. Only instead of brooms marching toward me, it's gay tourists, more and more and more of them."

Davor tried to snatch away the brandy decanter as his mother reached for it, but she was too quick for him. "Mother, you've been drinking far too much lately. I know you've been unhappy since the National Opera canceled your contract —"

"And who can blame me?" Vuksa cried. "First a shift from leads to character roles, then a push into the chorus, then a shove over to the supernumeraries. But from there to be booted into the superannuated, that was too much to bear." She wiped some tears from her eyes, though another sip of brandy restored her to calm. "We call this *orahovača*, darling Cliff. Can you say that?"

"Or-a-ho-va-cha," he pronounced carefully.

"Your ear is excellent! You're making such good progress with our language."

Davor noted that Gaydonia wasn't the only thing making strange bedfellows of these two. More interested in Zablvacia's past than its present, Cliff had been inspired to write a play in blank verse about one of its early kings. This was Ivan the In-effectual, famous for inviting the Turks to drop by the country whenever they liked, thinking this would be good for trade. Cliff assured Vuksa that the role of Ivan's mother, which he described as Lady Macbeth and the Three Witches rolled into one, would be perfect for her.

Over the next few days, Davor and Ivo came up with a plan to secure the allegiance of at least the two waverers, Marija and Nevenka. At another dinner, Davor set this plan in motion. As soon as the family was seated at table, he clanged his fork against his empty wine glass to get everyone's attention.

"I have some exciting news. With Ranka's Good Enough scheme to contend with, Gaydonia mustn't neglect a single opportunity to make money. I've therefore devised a scheme to strengthen its lesbian angle."

Davor snatched up the hands of his wife and daughter, who were seated on either side of him. "Head Minister Petrak has agreed to send you two ladies abroad in search of an expert to help with the lesbian campaign."

Marija's green eyes lit up. "Where are we going? To London, New York?"

"Davor, can't I go, too?" Vuksa pleaded. "I have an affinity for lesbians. I once played Madam Butterfly as one. I killed myself out of love for my maid, Suzuki. The critics agreed it was a striking interpretation."

"I thought you were against Gaydonia, Mother."

Vuksa shrugged. "I could be bribed into temporary co-operation."

"Or to Paris?" Marija beamed. "Oh Davor, I haven't visited Paris since our honeymoon."

Davor cleared his throat apologetically. "Gaydonia has a very limited budget, so I'm sending you somewhere closer and cheaper. To the very birthplace of lesbianism, the home of the poetess Sappho, the sun-kissed island of Lesbos. It's a pilgrimage site for gay women from all over the world."

Nevenka and Marija looked dubious. "The island – of Lesbos?" they said together.

Vuksa leaned back in her chair. "Never mind."

Chapter 7

A week later, Marija was riding a motor-scooter along a bumpy dirt road on the sun-kissed island of Lesbos, Nevenka seated behind her. The mid-day sun bore down upon them out of an intensely blue sky, and they wore shorts, sandals, and sunglasses. As far as they were aware, they hadn't talked with a single lesbian during their entire time on the island. They were hampered in their efforts by speaking hardly any Greek. Marija had been relying on Nevenka for this, since she'd managed so well in Crete on a recent trip with school friends. Nevenka countered that while she was fine in any situation covered by her phrasebook, that didn't include tracking down lesbian hangouts. "Where are the women together?" was the best she could do, and the farmer they'd questioned back at the crossroads had pointed in this direction.

"So far, we haven't seen anything except a lot of olive trees and some tortoises moving faster than we are," Marija complained.

"We're coming to the water," Nevenka said as a line of blue appeared between the trees. "Maybe we'll find something there."

"This is another wild goose chase," Marija said as they looked up and down the sandy beach. "There's no one at all here, let alone a flock of lesbians."

Nevenka pointed off to the left. "Look, Mother, at the other end. Aren't those tents?"

Yes, they were tents, the two women discovered as they drew nearer, eight or nine family-sized ones grouped together below a cliff. Tents, but apparently without inhabitants. Advancing cautiously, Nevenka called out in Greek, "*Hallo! . . . Hallo!*" They moved toward the unzipped flap of one tent. Before they could look inside, a woman, moving with scarcely a sound over the sand, whipped up from behind and barred the way. She was entirely naked, bronzed by the sun and dripping wet, having apparently just emerged from the sea. She held a spear in a threatening pose, with a fish skewered on its tip.

"*Was wollen Sie hier?*" she demanded.

"Er," was all that emerged from Marija lips, her mind paralyzed by the sight of the spear.

The woman spoke again, now in heavily-accented English. "What do you want?"

"We are – like you," Marija improvised. "We are women who love women. We are looking for other women who love women." She gestured at Nevenka. "This is my – my partner. *Meine Frau.*"

The German Woman prowled around Marija and Nevenka, scrutinizing them. Meanwhile other women, also brown and bare-skinned, appeared from between the flaps of the tents or seemingly materialized out of the sand and water.

"You do not belong here," the German Woman growled. "You are not one of us. We come here every spring. We live off the land. Simply and in harmony with nature, as people did when they worshiped Gaia, the earth goddess, she of the ample breasts."

The women formed a circle around the intruders. "How interesting," Marija stammered. She looked around for a possible means of escape and found none. "Please do go on."

The German Woman shook her spear angrily, making the fish at its end flap about. "We live as our ancestors did before treacherous men seized power and the Dark Ages of Patriarchy began. Patriarchy, with its endless turmoil and oppression and environmental degradation. You are pale and weak-looking. You do not know how to spear fish or make fire."

"That's not true. We are – strong women. We worship Gaia, the ample-breasted goddess. We want the same things you do."

The woman took two enraged steps toward Marija. "You want what I have? You want my fish, my shelter, my woman?"

Nevenka whispered, "Mother, it's no use pretending. You're only getting us in trouble."

Her role as Gaydonian publicist having worn off some of Nevenka's shyness, she squared her teenage shoulders and addressed the German Woman boldly. "The truth is, my mother is a psychologist, and we've come to the sun-kissed island of Lesbos to research lesbian lifestyles. How you like to spend your leisure time. What –" Nevenka looked around at the primitive camp – "what amenities you value when you travel."

The woman lowered her spear. "You do not want my shelter or my fish or my woman?"

"No, we only wish to talk. To dream with you of a day when women will once again rule the earth with wisdom and compassion. When we'll pray to Gaia for forgiveness each time we pluck a root or leaf or fruit from her sacred body. When we'll stand on the necks of puny, sniveling, hairy, breastless men and show them their proper place in the world."

After a long silence, the German Woman said, "Very well, we shall talk with you." She gave a tug to the collar of Nevenka's short-sleeved blouse. "But first, you must divest yourselves of these stifling encumbrances foisted on you by the capitalist patriarchal system."

Exchanging a look that said, "It's all for the cause," Nevenka and Marija began to undress. . . .

By that evening, they were enjoying a dinner of fried fish with the hardy band of naturalists. By that night, after large amounts of local wine, they'd managed to interest the German Woman, Wilhelmina Schmautz, in Gaydonia, and she agreed to return with them to Zablvacia. "I am determined that this not be yet another enterprise dominated by the Male," she declared.

Davor wasted no time in making use of Fraulein Schmautz. The day after her arrival, he convened a meeting in the Grand Salon of all the Ministers of Finance assigned to Gaydonia, joined by Ivo and Marija. He pointed out to the ministers that the Chestnut Blossom Festival in mid-May, the starting point of the Gaydonia tourist season, was fast approaching.

"Ivo and I know you've all worked hard preparing for your roles as faux gays. You've already spent countless hours watching videos and reading material we've assigned, as well as practicing among yourselves. However, we believe one final training session is required to achieve complete success. We're most fortunate to have as a guest instructress Wilhelmina Schmautz, who will work with the female ministers."

Dressed in a becoming beige hemp pants-suit, Fraulein Schmautz gave a curt nod of acknowledge.

"The male ministers will be under the supervision of my son Ivo and. . ." Davor looked toward Ivo to see whether he could add Cliff's name. Ivo had been pleading with Cliff earlier that morning for help with this endeavor, which fell right within his expertise of Theater Arts. After checking the

messages on his mobile, Ivo shook his head at Davor to in-
dicate that Cliff hadn't changed his mind at the last minute.
Davor finished his sentence with, "And I'm sure he'll do an
excellent job."

Davor had the male and female ministers stand in separate lines. Fraulein Schmautz and Ivo paced up and down like
two generals inspecting their troops while the ministers eyed
them with apprehension.

Davor addressed the ministers. "These two experts will ad-
vise you about – well, whatever it is that goes into making gay
people appear gay. Diet, hair, make-up, clothes, deportment."

Fraulein Schmautz stroked her chin, looking over the dis-
taff contingent. "This will take much time and effort."

"I can assure you, Fraulein," Davor said, "these are men
and women accustomed to hard work."

"Let us begin at once. You two will wait outside, please,"
she said, waving a hand at Davor and Marija. "We must have
no distractions."

Davor and Marija withdrew to the hall, where they sat
on a seat in a bay window. From here, they had a side view of
the clock tower. Ten o'clock arrived, and the soldier, scientist,
laborer, and other figures swung jerkily out of one door below
the clock and disappeared into another. Eleven o'clock, and
they emerged again. At noon, the golden cockerel, the only
feature salvaged from the medieval original, popped out of a
door above the clock and crowed twelve times, extending its
golden neck.

The afternoon passed, then the evening. Through the
closed doors of the Grand Salon, Davor and Marija could hear
the voices of Ivo and Fraulein Schmautz, at times low and per-
suasive, at other times raised, hectoring. Diverse sounds came
from the ministers: sighs, laughs, shrieks, sobs.

Finally, at almost two in the morning, when Davor and Marija had drifted into uneasy sleep on the window seat, Fraulein Schmautz and Ivo flung open the doors to the Salon and summoned them inside. Davor and Marija found the ministers standing in two rows again. Davor and Marija circled them, studying them carefully. Ivo and Fraulein Schmautz hovered to one side with triumphant expressions, like two great artists presenting their masterpiece.

"Davor," Marija whispered, "the ministers seem exactly the same to me."

"And to me," Davor whispered back. "We must not know what to look for." To Fraulein Schmautz and Ivo, he enthused, "What an amazing transformation! I don't know how to thank you. . . ."

Chapter 8

Preparations for Gaydonia soon reached fever pitch. At the border posts, down came the drab black-and-white Zablvacia signs, which seemed to say, "We wish you were somewhere else and probably you do, too." Up went flashy purple-on-pink Gaydonia ones that shouted, "Lucky you, you're about to enter a land of excitement and adventure!" Rainbow flags appeared everywhere, fluttering from rooftops and along the town walls, draped over building facades, with holes cut in them so people could see out their windows. Nevenka dashed off rainbow designs for everything from bus transfers to postage stamps to the floral beds in Pupina Square. Late into the night, one could hear the voices of the ministers drift out of the Town Hall, where they sat in a language lab practicing how to say in a variety of languages, "I'm here with my boyfriend/girlfriend."

With Davor and Ivo tirelessly stoking the Gaydonia advertising engine, posters sprang up in travel agencies around the world showing smiling same-sex couples posed in Zablvacian locales. In the interests of thrift and expediency, the couples were actually Davor and Ivo, Marija and Nevenka. Off in Taipei or Toulouse or Timbuktu, who was to know? The posters asked, "Gaydonia, is it the new Shangay-La?" Apparently people wanted to find out, for hotel reservations poured in.

Leaping from one triumph to another, it nagged at Davor that the two most vehement remaining critics of Gaydonia were part of his circle of intimates: his mother and Cliff.

Davor and Ivo came up with another plan. Returning to their building on the evening they were to put it into effect, they heard Vuksa's voice coming from the other side of the front door.

What monstrous rumor ripples through the court?
Our city gates you'd open to the Turks?

Followed by Cliff's.

Dear Mother, do not fear the Turkish hordes.
Their ways are most refined, their only thoughts
Of art, and dainty foods, and fleshly love.
No taste have they for violence, save for this,
They doff their clothes and slick their parts with oil,
And tight entwined will wrestle on for hours.

"Oh no!" Ivo moaned. "They're rehearsing *Ivan the Ineffectual* yet again."

Davor observed, "Some plays are tragedies, and some it's a tragedy they were ever written."

Soon everyone was converging on the dining table, except Davor, who was at work in the kitchen.

"How's my favorite Zablvacian?" Cliff asked, sitting down beside Ivo.

"Fine," Ivo answered, in a not-fine tone.

"Okay, baby doll, what's the matter?"

"I'll tell you. The Chestnut Blossom Festival and the unveiling of Gaydonia are only a week away. We've still got a million things to do, and I wish my boyfriend could spare some time to help."

"Cupcake, the further Gaydonia emerges from its shell, the less I like the look of it."

"People here will suffer real hardships if we can't repay those World Bank loans. The sort a pampered American like you can only imagine."

Vuksa, whose memory wasn't what it used to be, had brought her script to the table. "'What dreadful rumor rages through the court?'" She checked the page. "Damn! 'What monstrous rumor ripples. . . ?'"

"It's a terrible blow." Marija was consoling Nevenka for the shocking news that had reached them earlier that day. The factory in Bangkok making the Gaydonia condoms she'd designed had been almost completely destroyed by a mysterious explosion, scattering condoms as far away as Phuket. "And they were so lovely, extending to show a full-color illustration of the clock tower."

"Father thinks it may be sabotage. That terrible Ranka Vilović —"

At that moment, Davor burst into the room and set down a casserole dish on the table. Marija leaned toward it, sniffing. "Davor, is this your famous podvarak?"

"Yes, my precious, made with extra garlic and lots of paprika, just the way you like." He dished her up. "Here are some especially large pieces of pork for my dear wife."

"Davor," Marija said, "the most wonderful thing happened today. I saw three new patients in my private practice. Not one, not two, but three. And it's all thanks to Gaydonia. Everyone wants to talk about gay this and gay that, hope, fear, love, hate."

Vuksa assumed the look of searing disapproval she'd found useful throughout her career, both on stage and, in negotiations over her contract, backstage as well. "Shame on you, Marija, exploiting all the mischief Gaydonia has stirred up in people's heads. Which reminds me, Davor, there's the matter of directions."

"What do you mean, 'directions'?" he asked.

"Once those odious gay tourists arrive, I want to make it clear I will not give any of them directions."

"Mother, I'm surprised you don't look more kindly on gay people. I understand they're eager to crowd into theaters to see performers no one else will. Performers who are, shall we say, a little past their prime."

Vuksa gave her heavily penciled eyebrows a sarcastic tilt. "Unfortunately, no one has arranged for me to appear in a theater into which such people might crowd."

"Ivo, I think it's time we share with the family our good news."

"We've persuaded the Stupnik Theater to stage a Gaydonia Folkloric Evening," Ivo announced. "The program will include a scene from Clifford Tillman's new play, Nevenka Matošić performing on the violin, and vocal works by Madam Ćuruvija."

"My play!" Cliff kissed Ivo on the side of his head with a loud smack. "Ivo, you big sweetheart."

"Oh my God," Nevenka cried, both scared and excited, "to perform in front of all those people!"

As for Vuksa, she rose from her seat in an ecstatic trance. "The Stupnik! Finally to return there after all this time. That peculiar scent compounded of beeswax and old woodwork. The red velvet curtain parting with a *woosh*. The poky little dressing rooms backstage, the funny old man who manages the stage door. The Stupnik, where the luminaries of Zablvacia's Golden Age trod the boards: Krešimir Cosic, Anica Isakov, Gordana Rukavina. What shall I perform? The tessitura of *The Serpent*

Bridegroom is beyond me now. Except perhaps for my final aria, 'Coiling and Recoiling.' That's placed rather low."

Ivo said gently, "Gran, this is a folkloric evening. A simple folk song would be best."

"Whatever you say, dear boy. The simplest of simple folk songs, sung with touching sincerity." Vuksa clasped his hands. "Thank you for this chance to make a – what's the word?"

"A come-back, Gran."

Vuksa nodded. "So that's how it is. Gay people come out, and old performers come back." She started to move away from the table.

"Gran, where are you going?" Nevenka said. "You haven't finished your dinner – or your brandy."

"I must find a map of the city. I need to burn it into my brain so that no matter where one of those delightful gay tourists wants to go, I can give him the clearest, most accurate directions. As for this," Vuksa said, taking up her half-filled glass, "I swear not to touch another drop of liquor until after my engagement."

Davor leaned toward Ivo. "It's just like it says in the old Zablvacian proverb: 'You can catch a bear with a trap, but a honey pot is better.'"

The evening before the Chestnut Blossom Festival was one of strange beauty and calm, as if, following its exertions over the last month, the country was enjoying a brief, final moment of repose. After dinner, the family walked to the River Tav to see the chestnut trees lining its banks. Performing their patriotic duty, these were covered with white blossoms. The full moon was like a lamp held up to light the family's way.

Davor and Marija were in front. Davor was saying, "And who made it possible for his dear wife to resign from her dreary job at the Ministry of Health and devote all her energies to her private practice?"

"Is it really happening?" Marija beamed. "Will I never have to counsel parents who beat their children or men who expose themselves in public ever again?"

"No, you'll only have to deal with high-functioning neurotics like me. Gaydonia has made all our dreams come true."

They approached a stone bridge. At the near end, they found a middle-aged woman in native costume singing a melancholy folk song.

> *Na me pogled tvoj obrati*
> *I ti vidi me na mire.*
> *Vidi vidi jednom krati*
> *Koj' za tobom sved umire.*

As they passed, Davor and Marija dropped some coins into the hat at the woman's feet. They paused to lean on the balustrade, looking down at the white moon mirrored in the black water.

Marija fingered the heart on the chain around her neck, the heart Davor had given her. "Remember when we heard the Haydn mass at St. Stephan's last Christmas?" she said. "The women would sing a phrase, then the men would sing it, as if they were bending over them. It made me think of you and me coming together, our two voices, our bodies."

Davor took her hand. "Did it, my love?"

"I'm happy Cliff came into Ivo's life. I'm happy about Gaydonia and the way the family has worked together to make it happen. But it still makes me sad to think Ivo will never have that experience, the man and the woman coming together, en-twining."

"Male voices can sound wonderful together, too, Marija."

Marija took Davor's face between her hands and kissed him once. "That was for you." She kissed him again. "And that was for me."

A short ways behind them strolled Ivo and Cliff. They, too, dropped some coins in the singer's hat, then paused partway across the bridge. The evening was so still, they could hear the river whispering to itself below.

Cliff looked back at the singer. "That's such a beautiful song."

"It's even more beautiful when you know what she's saying."

"I do know. She's saying, 'The river speaks, and we are silent. The river moves, and we are still. . . .'"

Ivo was about to protest that those weren't the right words, then caught himself and let Cliff continue with his invented lyric.

"'May a time never come, my love, when I look down from this bridge and see only my own face in the water.'"

The bridge witnessed another moonlight kiss.

Nevenka and Vuksa brought up the rear. A Vuksa with no scent of walnut brandy on her breath, her make-up carefully applied, walking with a lighter step than usual. Coins from Nevenka made a *chink* as they fell into the singer's hat, unac-companied by ones from her grandmother.

"She's not bad, that singer." Vuksa put a hand to her hair, which had recently undergone an alchemical transformation from iron gray to purist gold. "Though just a touch flat."

"She sounds so alone," Nevenka said, "singing by herself. She reminds me of how I sometimes sing to myself when I'm afraid."

"Piffletosh," Vuksa said, "what do you have to be afraid of, a healthy, talented young girl like you?"

Nevenka looked down at the river, where the water was trying to carry away the reflected moon, always without success. "I'm afraid of living in such a small country, for one thing. My science teacher says we live on a small unimportant planet in a small unimportant solar system. And I think, I live in a small, unimportant country, too. At night, I lie in bed and worry that it's getting even smaller. Eroding, like that island." She gazed at a grassy little island in the middle of the river, shaped like a rough-edged boat.

"Sometimes if I watch that island long enough," Nevenka continued, "I see a piece of soil break off and slip into the water. I'm afraid our country will disappear like that, bit by bit, and all of us will disappear with it, my family, my friends. So I sing to myself just to make sure my piece of soil is still holding on."

In a rare moment of grandmotherly warmth, Vuksa put her arm around Nevenka's narrow shoulders. "We're not so insignificant anymore, are we? Why, people all over the world are talking about Gaydonia. So please save your singing for pleasant moments in the shower."

Chapter 9

At last, the day of the Chestnut Blossom Festival arrived, and the gay tourists started flooding in. They came by train and bus if they lived nearby, in Croatia, Serbia, Romania; by plane at the minuscule Zablvacian airport if they had a greater distance to cover. Men, women, singles, couples, groups, young and old and in between, decked out with sunglasses and cameras and backpacks. The visitors were greeted by clusters of schoolchildren who sang a specially composed song of welcome. Grabbing Nevenka's Gaydonia map, they dashed off to see the sights, such as they were.

"The tourists seem to be enjoying themselves," Nevenka wrote that afternoon to her Chilean pen-pal, who had revived their correspondence after obscure Zablvacia was replaced by the instantly notorious Gaydonia. "Well why not, they're on vacation. Gaydonia probably isn't the most beautiful or interesting place they've ever seen, but Father says tourists are used to being disappointed. The reality never lives up to the glossy photographs and lyrical descriptions. And there are a lot of other gay people around, which according to him is really all you can expect from a place called Gaydonia."

People jammed the sidewalks to watch the Chestnut Blossom Festival procession, tourists and locals cheek by jowl.

Later came the first Folkloric Evening at the Stupnik Theater, the opening night audience crowding through the doors.
Against a painted backdrop of Zablvacian woodlands, Cliff
and Vuksa acted a scene from *Ivan the Ineffectual.* Their costumes were medieval, their acting technique only slightly more
up-to-date, and they were met with applause that wasn't much
louder than the first few drops of a summer shower. The ministers performed a graceful Scarf Dance, the women wearing
brightly embroidered skirts, the men in vests and breeches.
This produced a response more like a sturdy winter downpour.

When the curtain opened again, it was on a dark stage.
A spotlight snapped on, revealing Nevenka. She wore a Little
Black Dress that exposed as much of her slender figure as it
covered, and she clutched a violin in one hand, a bow in the
other. She seemed immobilized by the row upon row of expectant faces. On the sidelines, Vuksa held her breath. Yet
some of her theatrical blood must have flowed in her grand-
daughter's veins, for after a moment Nevenka tucked the violin
under her chin and launched into a dazzling gypsy-flavored
solo. The audience murmured its appreciation of her showy
runs and double-stops and pizzicati.

A pause, then three more spotlights picked out Davor,
Ivo, and Marija, who accompanied Nevenka on the mandolin,
bagpipe, and *dumbek*, a local type of drum. The music sped up
into a lively folk song with a steady beat.

One could sense the audience's mounting excitement, but
there was still more to come. Propelled by Cliff and several
stage-hands, a plaster hillock slid onto the stage with Vuksa
seated regally on top. The sequins covering her sapphire blue
evening gown flashed with her least movement. Standing to
her full five-foot-three height, with the song now a full-throttle
folk-pop number, she belted the lyrics. Vuksa had written these

herself, simply reordering the words of the current top ten songs, such as *love, want, oh* and *ah*. As a sign of welcome to her international audience, she used a variety of languages. Reviewers later singled out her Hungarian for special praise.

Vuksa glided down the path on the front of the plaster hill and performed a dance with the ministers that involved leaps and spins remarkable for someone her age. As the ministers carried her off stage on their shoulders in a horizontal position, the audience made a roar like a once in a lifetime deluge.

Late that night, after the petals dropped from tossed bouquets had been swept off the stage of the Stupnik, while the new bars and cafes on Pupina Square were emptying, as the vendor selling tutti frutti ice cream was at last wheeling his cart home, a dark bulky figure slipped into the Town Hall. It was Davor. After checking some numbers in a notebook, he approached a large chart that stood in the foyer. This looked something like a double thermometer, with marks on each one representing increments of a hundred thousand kunars. He shoved the rainbow flag emblem on the left side up a few inches, then made a derisive face at the cookie emblem on the right.

Upstairs, seated at his desk, Davor attended to a few matters that were weighing on his mind. Then he leaned back in his chair and gazed at the circle of cherubs in the fresco overhead. Reaching up his stubby-fingered hands as if to take hold of theirs, he let the chair spin slowly round and round.

Chapter 10

Four months passed. The tourists came and went, spent and spent, and the rainbow emblem on the chart inched ever upward. Ranka's profits rose steadily, too, though never by leaps and bounds. After all, the selling point of her products was that they didn't inspire much enthusiasm. Still, when Davor hoped the rustic resort he was opening on the River Tav would give Gaydonia a strong lead, Ranka brought out *The Good Enough Cookbook* with recipes for dishes like Eggs Benedict Arnold, Oysters on the Quarter Shell, and Pigs in Sheets, and her fortunes improved as well.

By mid-September, the trees on the hillsides to the north and south of the city were tinged with fall colors. A hint of autumnal gold could be detected in the warm sunlight pouring onto Svetorgska Street one afternoon as the Matošić family strolled along it, their eyes shielded by sunglasses. Davor wore an off-white linen suit, and its Italian makers combined with some dieting gave him a more slender appearance. In fact, the entire family sported stylish new clothes. The change was most striking in Nevenka, who wore a Mondrian-esque outfit of black lines and primary colors, along with hip boxy glasses; and in Vuksa, dressed in a white silk dress sprinkled with red polka dots and carrying a red parasol.

A hawker for one of the many restaurants on the street tried to press menus on the family. "*Wir haben bei uns gut Essen. Beaucoup choses à manger.* We have many tasty things to eat."

"No, thank you," they all murmured. "We've already had lunch. We're just passing."

The only one in the group who wasn't better dressed was Cliff, who wore the drab, droopy clothes of the old-style Zablvacians.

"I remember my first Sunday here," he sighed. "Only a few people in the streets, the sound of church bells everywhere. Now I can barely hear the bells over the tourist ruckus."

Marija stopped in front of a tourist shop and picked through the items on display, Gaydonia tablecloths, placemats, tea cozies, playing cards, beach blankets, puzzles, mugs, calendars. "We've got everything a visitor needs," she observed dryly.

"The fountains are running thanks to tourist money," Ivo said, gesturing to one in a small square.

"That one is running," Nevenka complained, "but I can hardly see it behind that stand advertising eight-inch wieners."

Davor adjusted his Panama hat at a jaunty angle. "We're restoring St. Stephan's Cathedral at last, and the Mosque."

"Yes," Vuksa said, giving her parasol a vexed twirl, "so tourists in shorts and tank tops can go inside and take lots of pictures of things they don't understand."

At that moment, two tourists in just such outfits accosted them, one blond, the other brunet, but otherwise difficult to distinguish. "Hey, excuse me," the blond one said, "can you tell us how to get to Pupina Square?"

The brunet giggled. "Yeah, we're kind of lost. These little winding streets are real cute, but they've got us all twisted around."

The family smiled at them wearily, all except Vuksa, who examined her red fingernails.

"Keep going down this street," Davor said, pointing. "You can't miss it."

"Gee, thanks a lot!" the visitors cried. "That's really nice of you. Have a super great day."

"Let's face it," Ivo said after the family had walked on a ways, "we've entered the Age of the Tourist. We're all visitors now. Onlookers, voyeurs. We're part of glob-ilization, in which every place in the world becomes part of an indistinguishable glob."

"I refuse to accept that," Cliff frowned.

"You don't want there to be no tourists here, Cliff. You just want to be the only one."

"I don't want to be a tourist. I'm learning your incredibly difficult language. I've bought Zablvacian clothes. I want to fit in."

Ivo planted a big kiss on his mouth. "Remember, I couldn't do that in Zablvacia, but I can in Gaydonia."

They passed a poster advertising the last Gaydonia Folkloric Evening of the season. Nevenka exclaimed, "If I have to see the ministers perform the Scarf Dance one more time –"

Marija chimed in, "If I pass another man in the street who doesn't look at me and another woman who does –"

Followed by Vuksa, "If someone asks me for directions to Pupina Square again, *in English* –"

A street merchant lunged toward them offering two pairs of same-sex puppets holding hands. "Take your pick, the boyfriend puppets or the girlfriend puppets. Extra special price today only."

"No, thanks. . . . Not now. . . Not interested."

"The tourists have revived your career, Gran," Ivo pointed out. "You have your own cabaret act in the revolving bar atop the new Hilton. You should be grateful."

Another parasol twirl. "Gratitude is a difficult emotion to sustain."

"The tourists aren't doing my career any good," Cliff grumbled. "The full-length version of *Ivan* has been a complete flop."

"Cliff," Ivo said, "the problem is that your play is a stinker, not that people can smell the stink."

"Now, now you two," Davor said, "let's not spoil our afternoon with quarreling. We hardly ever get to spend time together like this anymore, we're all so busy."

"And we know why that is!" Vuksa cried. "It's true what they say about gay people threatening family values. Gaydonia has taken my family away from me."

They emerged into Pupina Square, which was now littered with snack stands, sketch artists, mimes. Folk musicians played on one side, a rock group on another, their music clashing. Tourists milled among the milling pigeons, snapping photographs. A gold-painted go-go-boy in a cage beckoned some passersby into a gay guy bar, while a go-go girl tried to lure two women into a lesbian one a few doors down.

With so many distractions, it wasn't surprising the family almost collided with Head Minister Petrak as he strayed across the square, deep in thought.

"It's the Matošić family," he exclaimed, "out in full force! Or are only some of you 'out'?" He chuckled at his own joke, then turned to Marija. "Dr. Matošić, how is your private practice coming along? Are all your patients still chattering on about gay this and that?"

"No, Head Minister," Marija smiled, "the gay thing has become old hat. They've all gone back to complaining about their unhappy childhoods."

"Nevenka, I hardly recognize you," Petrak said. "You've become such a smart-looking young lady."

Nevenka simpered in her terribly cool outfit. "I've become chums with one of the visitors, Calvin St. de la Coco Croix, and he's convinced me to become a fashion designer instead of a violinist."

Petrak's wandering gaze lit on Vuksa. "And Madam Ćuruvija, looking more radiant than ever. You're a poem, a symphony, a goddess."

The maneuvers of the red parasol were coquettish now. "Head Minister, I don't know whether to rhyme, or crescendo, or make you worship me on your knees."

"To have you back at the Stupnik – it's been like old times. I've attended every one of your performances."

"Have you, Head Minister?"

"Call me Slavko, please. And I'll call you Vuksa, if I may."

"Of course."

"Vuksa, when I first admired you, I was a shy young man, and at present I'm an only somewhat less shy old man. But after all these years, there's something I must ask. Would you – would you do me the honor of dining with me after your next performance?"

"Why, Head Minister – Slavko! I'd be delighted."

Petrak kissed Vuksa's hand, permitting his lips to linger. Then he gestured around him. "What do you think of your handiwork, Davor?"

"Head Minister, I'm happy about the money Gaydonia is bringing in –"

"And so you should be. Gaydonia seems sure to reach the five million kunars mark in just a few more days."

"But I have to admit, I'm looking forward to the end of the tourist season. A little peace and quiet –"

"Davor, there's the winter season to consider. Same-sex ski lifts, pink triangle runs."

Davor opened his mouth to protest, then refrained. "Of course, Head Minister."

Petrak started to walk away, then caught himself. "Oh Davor, the Haunted Church ride in the amusement park still has some bugs to be worked out. I left a report on your desk."

"The auto-da-fé tableau still too realistic?"

"Yes, another tourist had his clothing singed only yesterday. Please look into the matter at once."

After Petrak left, Nevenka took her father's arm. "Do you really have to go to the office?"

"Just for a little while. Ivo, you'd better check things out at the park. I'll meet you there later."

Sitting at his desk in the Town Hall, Davor started to read the report with a mix of boredom and fatigue, then threw it down unfinished.

"Davor?" The low voice behind him made him wheel round in his chair. It was Ranka, her usual wry smile curving her lips.

"What are you doing here on a Sunday?" he asked.

"Working, like you.

With victory in sight, Davor could afford to be magnanimous. "You've put a lot of blood and sweat into Good Enough."

"And Gaydonia – what an amazing achievement!"

"Your saying that means a lot to me."

"Can I say something else? No, I'd rather show you."

Ranka led Davor to her desk, on top of which rested a huge sack overflowing with letters. She told him to take one. Pulling out a letter at random, he read aloud, "'Dear Ranka, with the help of Good Enough, I've shed nearly sixty pounds.'

What are these?" he asked, pointing at some marks on the page. "They look like drops of water."

"They're tears, Davor. Tears of gratitude for the mediocre manna I've brought into some chubby soul's life." Ranka reached into the sack. "Here, read some more."

Soon the voices of weight-losers from all over the globe were swirling around Davor.

I've now got a body I never knew I could have. . . .

My wedding ring finally fits again. . . .

Getting into restaurant booths is no longer an issue. . . .

My outlook on life has changed. And I tell everyone it's thanks to Good Enough.

Davor stopped reading and gave Ranka a long look. "Where is this leading?"

"I want you to let Good Enough win the contest."

Davor's mouth fell open. "You must be crazy!"

"Davor, think of all the benefits Good Enough brings."

"What about Gaydonia?"

"Which are there more of in the world, fat people or gay ones? And some gay people are fat, too. There's a cross-over."

Davor's thoughts took a more personal turn. "You used to complain I was dull, Ranka. A dull little apparatchik. Am I still dull, after dreaming up all this?"

He strode to a window and threw it open. The sounds of Gaydonia flooded in – voices, music, laughter. Ranka joined him, looking out.

"I admit it," Ranka said. "After Gaydonia, you glitter like the golden cockerel who crows every day at noon in the Town Hall clock tower."

"For once in my life, I, Davor Matošić, had a daring, brilliant idea," he exclaimed, pounding his bearish hands on his big chest, "and you want me to kill it off."

"Yes. At times we have to do things that are painful, for the sake of something more important."

Davor knew she was thinking of his breaking off their engagement twenty years ago so that he could marry Marija instead. "But you don't need to win the contest to go on with Good Enough. You can use your own money."

Ranka gave a single pained intake of breath. "Gone. All gone."

Davor's eyes grew wider. "The Pluzinova Cookie fortune? You sank the whole thing into Good Enough?"

"You know how little money Petrak gave to our projects, the old skinflint. The expenses kept mounting. Even mediocrity comes at a price nowadays." Ranka shook her head bitterly. "I wish I'd never started Good Enough. It's ruined me. My only hope is more government support. A big infusion this time."

Stunned by this revelation, Davor lifted his eyes to the ceiling. The ring of cherubs gazed down at him. Such was the genius of Giovanni Sottobosco that every time Davor looked at them, their expressions appeared subtly different, depending on his emotional state. At this moment, they seemed expectant, questioning.

"I can't make a decision without consulting Ivo," Davor said after a few minutes of rumination. "Gaydonia is his creation as much as mine. If he says no, that's the end of the matter."

Davor and Ranka dragged the sack of letters to the flat, where, inevitably, the whole family got involved.

"Davor," Marija said, "listen to what this man wrote –"

"Father, this girl is only seventeen –"

"Have you seen these Before and After photos?" Vuksa marveled.

Davor turned a questioning look on his son, who was skimming letter after letter. "Ivo?" he said.

A long silence, with Ranka leaning forward, hands clasped before her.

At last, Ivo fixed Ranka with a deal-maker's gaze. "Ten percent of your profits to gay causes."

"Yes."

"And a blurb on every package saying as much."

"Done."

"My brilliant idea!" Davor couldn't help gasping as he saw it crumble before his eyes.

"You'll have other ones, Dad," Ivo said. "For a start, we can get to work on our project of creating a string of gay retirement homes. We've got an aging rainbow population to consider."

Davor bit a knuckle so hard, he almost broke the skin. "But even if we agree to get rid of Gaydonia, how can we? If I tell Petrak I resign, he'll just appoint another minister to run the show."

Judging from the look on Vuksa's face, Davor wasn't the only member of the family with a knack for brilliant ideas.

"You want to put a stop to Gaydonia?" she said with a wicked smile. "Nothing could be easier. Leave it to me."

Chapter 11

The final Folkloric Evening seemed on the point of ending like every other. After the cast took a bow, in response to the tumultuous applause, Vuksa, as if surprised and half unwilling, agreed to sing an encore, accompanying herself on the mandolin. More applause, but just as the audience thought it was time to gather up its coats, she cried:

"How do you like it here in Shangay-La?" Settling back down in their seats, people bellowed with approval. "Excellent!" Vuksa returned, her sapphire gown shimmering as she stood. "Now that I know how you feel, I'd like to share my own thoughts on the subject."

A television crew for a gay cable station was filming the event live from in front of the stage, and Vuksa paused to consider whether to favor the camera on her left or her right. She'd never been able to decide which was her best side; they were both so striking.

"Poor and desperate, we've made the tourist king in our country. Only he's King Midas. He turns everything he touches to gold. But he also kills them, all the things he loves."

People in the audience exchanged puzzled glances.

A huge outdoor screen had been set up in front of the Town Hall to display the broadcast. A crowd stood watching as a story-high image of Vuksa continued, "You love the quaint little shop across from the cathedral? Presto change-o, now it's full of rubbishy souvenirs."

In Marseilles, two Frenchmen lounged together on a sofa. "You love the picturesque cafe by the river?" Vuksa questioned them from their television set. "Abracadabra, it's a tourist trap, and you can't even afford to eat there anymore."

The old lady was a little rude, the men agreed, though her gown was *très chic*.

Two women in Sao Paulo watched the broadcast while eating their dinner. "You come here to see us, and instead you mainly see one another," Vuksa went on. "Other tourists in your tourist uniforms. Everyone in tennis shoes and baseball caps, everyone carrying cameras, backpacks. Young, old, Germans, Japanese, Americans."

"*Santa Maria mãe de Deus*," one woman asked the other, "is this supposed to be funny?"

On little screens on the back of the seats in front of them, two Russian men on a jet high above Siberia peered at a tiny image of Vuksa as she said, "You people gathered here are a special category of tourists. Do you know why you've become our target group? Not because we love you."

"And you wanted us to visit Gaydonia next summer!" one of the men exclaimed to the other. "*Ni za što!*"

In a gay bar in Cape Town, Vuksa gazed out of a big video screen on the back wall. "No," she said, "I'm afraid you aren't loved any more here than you are back home. It's because we can't get anyone else to visit our boring, backward little country."

One of the men shouted, "Shut up, you old witch!" chucking the olive from his cocktail at the screen.

Back on the stage of the Stupnik, the audience was letting out boos and cat calls. Many people near the stage crumpled up their programs and hurled them at Vuksa. One man sacrificed, not the classic rotten tomato, but a perfectly good one purchased at a market earlier that day. The sapphire shimmer must have thrown off his aim, for the tomato missed its mark by several inches.

Vuksa concluded, "So I say, dear tourists, do me and yourselves a favor, go back to your own countries and leave me in peace in mine. I say, *Tourists Go Home!*"

The boos became deafening, but Vuksa only took a bow that was as deep as her gown permitted. The red velvet curtain of the Stupnik Theater closed with a *woosh*.

The outdoor screen in Pupina Square went white, then black. The spectators walked away, talking heatedly among themselves. The show was over.

The next day, newspapers all over the world hit the streets with headlines such as, GAYS GAG AT GAYDONIA GAFF, and below, an unflattering photograph of Vuksa caught with her mouth open mid-sentence.

On television, newscasters made announcements that began along the lines of, "Many of you have heard of the tiny Balkan country of Gaydonia. But things weren't so gay there last night when. . ."

Irate words flew back and forth over telephones and through texts. "Gaydonia is only after our money." "We know when we're not wanted." On a dating app, someone typed, "I'll see you at ten, big boy. Hey, and what do you think of this whole Gaydonia thing?"

On Facebook, clicking mice everywhere were unfriending Gaydonia. Twitter was aflutter. Travel agents tore down the now-controversial Gaydonia posters. In Washington, D.C., a dozen protesters circled in front of the beleaguered country's embassy, a building not much larger than a pretzel stand. With angry shouts, they waved signs saying DOWN WITH GAYDONIA, BOYCOTT GAYDONIA, and GAYDONIA SHMADONIA.

Back in Zablvacia, as gay tourists packed their bags and left the country in a huff, an emergency meeting was convened at the Ministry of Finance. It was agreed that Gaydonia must be abandoned at once, with a pending measure of censure in the United Nations a particular concern.

As in a film running backward, much that had been done was quickly undone. At the border posts, workers replaced the old Zablvacia signs – thank goodness, with typical lack of efficiency, they hadn't destroyed them yet. The statue of David was whisked out of the Hotel Kasina, the nudes in the National Gallery returned to their fig-leafed state, the pony ride freed of references to the Wild Gay West. Rainbow flags were yanked down; gardeners dug up the multi-colored flowerbeds. With looks of satisfaction, the old couple with the shop on Pupina Square swept from their shelves every last dildo and leather harness, replacing them with laundry soap and other respectable goods. Gaydonia was no more.

Did it leave not a single trace behind? The answer was no. The loans to the World Bank were repaid in full thanks in part to this bold touristic experiment, and a plaque was placed on the east wall of the Town Hall acknowledging the contribution of the international gay community to this effort. At the World Bank, one official would sometimes ask another, "Whatever happened to that guy who dreamed up the Gaydonia scheme – what was his name?"

Winter came early to Zablvacia that year. One chilly Sunday afternoon, with patches of snow visible among the bare trees on either side of the valley, the Matošić family could be seen riding their bicycles beside the River Tav. Davor and Marija were in front, with Ivo, Cliff, and Nevenka close behind. These last two were engrossed in a discussion of the costumes Nevenka was designing for a modern-dress revival of *Ivan the Ineffectual.*

Still farther back pedaled Vuksa and Head Minister Petrak. Petrak babbled endlessly about how beautiful Vuksa was and what a magnificent voice she had, with deviations when some other thought distracted him. Vuksa was kind enough to let the poor old man rattle on, saying nothing, only nodding and smiling.

About the Author

Gary Pedler has written two adult novels, a YA novel, two story collections, and, a little to his surprise, a play. A resident of San Francisco for longer than he cares to admit, Gary qualifies as a true Bay Area denizen. Yet after a recent escape from his white-collar wage slave job, he's spent much of his time rambling around the world and, of course, writing about everything he sees.

Gary's travel memoir *Couchsurfing: the Musical* is published by Adelaide Books, and his MG novel *Amy McDougall, Master Matchmaker* will appear in spring 2021 from Regal House. Find out more about Gary at www.garypedler.com.